Prisoners of War

Stuart L. Scott

For Terry

Stuart Scott

Moscow, Idaho

Prisoners of War

Stuart L. Scott
Moscow, Idaho

Published by
Stuart L. Scott
112 S. Main St.
Moscow, Idaho

CreateSpace Edition
ISBN# 978-1-7322468-2-9

Cover Design by: Damonza

Contents

Acknowledgements

This has been a labor of love. Thanks to my volunteer readers, and their tough love, especially Harley Wright, now gone. Also to Glen Lanier and my beloved wife Susan.

Finally a thank you for his tough love to playwright Sam Hunter; I'm proud to know him. When *POW* was only an idea, I asked Sam to write it for me. His short answer; "No, you need to write it." Thanks for the needed kick.

Prologue: San Francisco, 1981

A knock at my front door interrupted the six o'clock news. My stomach contracted and my breathing slowed.

Today could be the day—the day that my past finally catches up with me! I listened for the sounds of heavy boots on the stairs, for the righteous pounding on the door, for the deep authoritative voice calling my name. I already knew how I could have been found out. With all these years to think about my crime, I'd realized my one mistake. Had they finally followed the faint dusty trail I'd left in my wake? I'd spent 35 years living with guilt about the damage I'd done and the men I may have killed. The fear of discovery left my soul and psyche brittle.

"Paperboy! Collecting for the Chronicle."

False alarm. This time, anyway. I paid for the past three months of deliveries. As I returned to the TV, Walter Cronkite's face filled the screen.

"Science and the spiritual met today in San Francisco's Langley-Porter Neuropsychiatric Institute at the University of California Medical Center. Researchers have unlocked the brain wave patterns of infants still in their mother's womb. At 23 weeks after conception the brain waves of unborn babies demonstrate rapid eye movements or REM sleep, which is characteristic of being in an active dream state. So, left for another day is the question: What does an unborn child dream about? And that's the way it is, March 6, 1981."

What filled my own head, though, were flashbacks during the day and dreams at night. Fifty-plus years of memories so vivid, so acute, I cannot escape them any longer.

I remember one particular Saturday evening. In a mere 25 days, I'd be married. Life seemed good—if not perfect—as I tapped the ashes from my pipe and closed out the day, December 6, 1941.

1.　　Keyport, December 7, 1941

It was late the next morning when I heard a commotion at the Olson house next door—crying and swearing. It sounded like a family fight, loud and vulgar even, yet personal. Sounds of confusion were also coming from the main gate at the nearby Keyport, Washington, Torpedo Station. I was used to the noise in the Keyport machine shop where I worked, building torpedoes for the Bureau of Ordinance. This was a different sound. Trucks were moving, people were shouting and booted feet were running. Behind me, through his closed door, I heard my roommate Duano's voice.

"God damn it, you guys!"

He emerged half-dressed with jeans and socks on, his shirt and shoes in hand.

"Sunday morning is supposed to be quiet. What is the problem with those assholes?"

"Come on. Get dressed, and we'll head over to the gate and see what's up."

We walked out past our neighbor's store and into the street. Up ahead, one of the many Marines standing around turned briefly to respond to our shouted question.

"What the hell's going on?"

"The Japs bombed our fleet at Pearl Harbor. We're at war."

His words stopped us both in our tracks. In the confusion at the main gate, I saw a familiar figure, Captain Olson, my landlord and chief of security at Keyport.

"Captain Olson! Is there something we should do to help? Just tell us what you need."

"Thanks, fellas. For now, it would be best for you just to go home until your next shift. If I need to organize work or defense parties, I'll send someone over to get you. Bad business, this."

Then Olson turned away to direct the makeshift barricade being erected outside the gate. Still stunned, Duano and I walked back to our house and sat down on the porch to watch the action at the main gate. I stepped inside and turned on the radio, hoping for, all the while dreading, more news.

The news was on every station. The few details available were being repeated and occasionally augmented when more information came in from across the Pacific. We didn't have a phone, so I tried calling home using the pay phone at the Keyport Mercantile. Again and again I turned the rotary dial, trying to call San Bruno. I tried my parents' house first and then my fiancée's home, but every attempt rang as a busy signal.

Walking away from the pay phone through the bright sun of this particular Sunday morning, I would never have believed that inside of two years I would become a traitor to my country.

* * *

On Monday every worker on shift arrived early, and a somber silence prevailed throughout the building. Each man was greeted upon arrival by his supervisor.

"There will be an announcement over the P.A. at 8 a.m., so don't bother to start work yet."

We understood and shared the mix of pain, outrage and fear that surrounded us all. Moving inside, we gathered in small knots—talking, many smoking—while we waited. Some of the men sat on the row of benches that ran down the center of each aisle of the locker room. I chose to go into the cavernous work room, preferring the cold morning light and familiar comfort of my own work station. Leaning on my workbench as I waited for the announcement, I was soon joined by Andy, who worked at the bench next to me. He nodded but didn't speak.

At precisely 8 a.m. a click came from the speakers mounted near the ceiling. Some of us turned to face the sound; others just looked up or stared off into space. Some never raised their eyes from the shiny, gray cement floor.

"Good morning. This is Commander Munson." His voice was steady and devoid of emotion, with an even pace that faltered only when he listed the casualties. "I have been instructed to read and then post the following cable from the War Department in Washington, D.C.

"Yesterday at just past 8 a.m. local time, naval forces of Japan conducted a surprise attack on elements of our Pacific Fleet at anchor in Pearl Harbor, Hawaiian Islands. Attacking in three waves, Japanese aircraft sunk or severely damaged eight battleships, three cruisers and three destroyers. Loss of aircraft by Marine and Army air-corps units at Hickam Field totaled two hundred sixty-two aircraft. Casualty figures are currently at two thousand killed or wounded with the final total expected to go higher. At 11:06 local time, President Franklin D. Roosevelt addressed Congress and, with only one dissent, Congress voted to declare war on Japan and empowered the president to wage war against Japan with all of the resources of the United States."

I could hear sobbing and cursing in the background. Some of the words were spit out clearly, others more swallowed by the speakers.

"Sons-a-bitches," cursed a faceless voice from the crowd.

Commander Munson spoke again after about 30 seconds of silence, though it seemed more like 30 minutes. "Gentlemen, you are a part of the 'full resources of the United States' that Congress and the president will now use to punish Japan for this cowardly attack. Much will be demanded of us all in the coming days, but I don't expect it to be more than what we can willingly give.

"You will be getting more information from your section leaders in a few moments. God bless you all and God bless the United States."

The P.A. speakers went silent. To a man, none of us moved. In that moment of our shared national outrage, I hated the Japanese as much as any man on the station. My hate for the Japanese arose from their attack on Pearl Harbor and its potential impact on my future. I feared the attack had sunk not only our ships, but also my plans. I worried that Bea, my Japanese-American fiancée, would suffer the effects of the collective hate and fear of our nation. I needed to let her know all was still right between us and we could survive the craziness that had overcome the world.

After a much longer silence, the voice of Bill Glasscock, our building supervisor, came over the speakers.

"Gentlemen, Commander Munson's orders are to expand production to the maximum extent possible. All leave has been cancelled. With the battleships out of action, our war in the Pacific, for the moment, will be largely dependent on submarines and carrier-based torpedo planes. Starting today, the work week will go from five days on, two days off to eight days on, two days off. Shifts will be extended from eight-to ten-hour days."

"There goes my wedding date," I said to Andy.

Glasscock continued. "Because of the vital nature of our work here at Keyport, physical security will be increased. Carry your photo ID badge with you at all times. We will be taking names of volunteers willing to be trained as a reserve force to defend the station should we come under attack. Sign-up sheets will be posted in the locker room. The station will be observing a mandatory blackout between twilight and dawn, starting today. Be on the lookout for suspicious persons inside and outside the station. Remember, information is a weapon for our enemy, so don't give him anything to use against us."

I passed through our locker room and joined the line already forming to volunteer for the station's auxiliary defense force. As I left the locker room with my lunch box in hand, I saw workmen installing footings outside the main door of the building.

"What's up, guy?"

"Blackout, pal. You don't want a Jap spy or bomber pilot to see light when you open the door at night, do yah? We're putting up another exterior door and a little walkway leading into the building. We'll have it done today, so don't worry."

Looking up over my left shoulder, I located the strange sounds that had caught my interest. Up on the roof, workmen were attaching heavy brown tarps. By the end of the shift— through the wall of windows that provided natural light for my delicate work—I saw the tarps descend. Blackout curtains—so we could work longer at making weapons to kill Japs, while the Japs supposedly looked for our tell-tale lights to sight their bombs or their deck guns. The curtains descending over our windows seemed to match the darkness covering the light in our once-sunny nation.

2.   San Bruno, 1920

I was a war baby, an only child. I'm Patrick Ellsworth McBride, born in 1920, almost exactly one year after my father came home from the war in Europe and married my mom. I grew up in San Bruno, a quiet suburb 10 miles south of San Francisco.

At the north end of San Bruno, on the east side of El Camino Real, was Tanforan Racetrack. The Twelfth Naval District Headquarters was directly across the street. Tanforan's huge grandstand backed onto El Camino Real. Red, white and blue pennants flew from what seemed like a million flag poles, lining the roof high above the chain-link fence that enclosed the grounds and parking lot.

The track was beautiful. The clean brown dirt surface was smoothed before each race like the infield of a baseball diamond. The infield was bordered by a low hedge circling the entire perimeter. Yellow marigolds and red petunias filled the track's infield space confined by the low green hedge. These stripes of floral color faced the grandstand and swept to the base of a green scoreboard in the center of the oval.

When I was old enough to ride a two wheeler, I'd leave home and ride my bike across town, turning at the tree-lined border of the Navy property. I loved to ride under the canopy of tall, fragrant eucalyptus that stood at regular intervals on my route. The oddly shaped leaves looked like flattened banana skins and had a rich camphor smell. Every part of the tree had the same strong medicinal odor, but it was especially strong on the leaves and acorns.

Behind the tree line I could see the cyclone fence of the naval property, rimmed with a necklace of barbed wire. Inside the fence, an asphalt road provided access to a long row of warehouses, each entered across a continuous cement loading dock. On the opposite side of the road lay barren ground, stretching north as far as I could see. The gentle roll of the ground—bright orange with California poppies—reminded me of a poem that my dad would recite to me.

"In Flanders fields the poppies blow."

Dad always followed the first line with a long pause.

"Where's Flanders, Dad?"

"It's a place in Belgium that I saw before you were born, son. The poem was written by a pal of mine, Johnny McCrae. He died in the war."

I would ride all around the outside of the Navy property and then turn south toward home. I'd stay on the wide flat surface of the El Camino Real and follow it to my right turn at Jenevein Avenue. Sakai's Garden Shop and Nursery marked the corner.

* * *

On September 10, 1926, Mom drove me to my first day of school. Her hand on my shoulder, we walked from the car to the door of the school. She asked if I could remember to take Bus number two home. I told her I would remember which bus to take. However, by the end of that first day, my mind went blank as I stood outside the school looking at the long line of buses. Mrs. Hailey, my teacher, crouched down and looked into my panicked face.

"Where do you live, honey?"

I was momentarily struck mute. I knew the answer, but a little round-faced girl spoke first. All I could do was stare down at the folded cuffs of my new Farah blue jeans.

"He lives on Chestnut Street," volunteered her small voice.

"Ah...is that right?" Mrs. Hailey asked me.

I nodded, and she led me by the hand to Bus number 2. My helper followed, getting on the same bus, and we sat side by side. As the bus drove along I studied our route, trying to find comfort in familiar streets. Occasionally I'd glance over at my companion. The pink ribbon in her hair matched the pink of her dress. Her shoes were white Mary Janes and her socks had little pink ruffles. Her name was Beatrice Sakai. She showed me where to get off at the Cherry Street stop. My sitter's home was in sight, just two houses up Cherry Street. I watched Bea walk another block up to Maple Street and vanish. Somehow, Bea knew me, but I didn't know her.

On the second day of school, my mom took me to the bus stop. Bea was there, so we rode together, silently sharing a seat. Riding the bus, and later, walking together to and from school with Bea became routine. If I wasn't waiting at the schoolyard gate to walk home, Bea questioned me about it the next day.

"Why weren't you here after school? Did you have to go to the principal's office?"

"Richard Salvi hit me with a rock at recess, and I went after him. The yard teacher saw me, and we both had to stay after school for fighting."

"You're not supposed to fight," she chided, imitating a disapproving adult.

"I just get so mad. I can't help it."

"My parents say it's not right to fight, unless it's to protect a lady or weak people who can't defend themselves."

Nothing more was said as we walked—until the next time I wasn't there to walk home with Bea.

* * *

Bea's father grew flowers over the hill from San Bruno in the coastal valley at Linda Mar. Mr. Sakai ran the flower field, growing yellow daffodils and white narcissus. They sold cut flowers and bulbs from a neat, wooden stand at the edge of the field, just off the Pacific Coast Highway, as well as from their garden shop in San Bruno.

Mrs. Sakai ran the garden shop with their son, Ernie, helping after school. Cool and shady, the shop's interior had an earthy smell that was a combination of soil and peat moss overlaid by the sharper tones of manure and fish emulsion. Above the heavier organic aroma wafted the sweet scent of the rose bushes, each in a five-gallon tin container awaiting purchase. The soft light of the interior, the visual beauty and the layered aromas all combined to give the shop an exotic feel. A service island filled the center of the room. A cash register adorned a tidy counter-top overlooking shelves of brown glass bottles. Fish emulsion, iron tonics and Black Flag bug killer were arranged neatly in rows that circled three sides of the counter. On the back of the shop was a lath house. The wood structure provided perpetual shade to pots of bulbs, camellias, rhododendrons and roses.

Watchfully seated on the shop floor was the Sakai family dog, Curley. The black-and-white cocker spaniel quietly policed the behavior of the clientele. His eyes followed Mrs. Sakai. If she walked from the shop into the lath house, he quietly followed. Any loud noise or talking near Mrs. Sakai and Curley would put himself between her and the source, a rumbling growl rising from deep in his chest.

Besides the shelves that held things either from or for the soil, there were two shelves of Japanese ceramic vases. One afternoon I watched Mom buying a new pair of cotton gardening gloves and admiring a particular terracotta-colored vase.

The front of the vase had been cut out to allow the inset of a delicately sculpted scene showing a miniature building inside the mouth of a natural grotto. Two trees with a million tiny leaves guarded the entrance to the grotto, adding depth to the sculpted image. Mom lusted over this one particular vase every time she went into the shop.

Mom's attention did not go unnoticed by Mrs. Sakai. She took the vase off the shelf and put it into my mom's hand.

"The vase depicts a famous Japanese shrine where ancient warriors sacrificed themselves in the service of their honor, staying loyal to their master even to their deaths."

10

I'd interrupted Mrs. Sakai. "What kind of guns did they have?"

"Patrick, you know not to interrupt." Mom looked at me, smiling as she spoke. "Please forgive him," she said to Mrs. Sakai.

"No, the masterless Samurai, who are now known as Ronin, did not have any guns. They each had two swords, one long and one short," said Mrs. Sakai, speaking directly to me.

"The swords were...very sharp!" She flared her eyes wide for emphasis, and I flinched and gasped in surprise.

"Were they good guys or bad guys?" I asked, ignoring a small jerk from my mother's hand that rested on my shoulder.

"Patrick, they were both good and bad at the same time. They were fighting their feudal governor, who was like their government, so in this way they were bad. But the governor was evil. They were fighting for somethings more important—their honor and duty to their lord. When you are older, you will maybe understand how loyalty and honor sometimes must struggle with our duty and obligations. This is how people can be both good and bad."

* * *

When I was a kid, Sunday was our father-son day. I'd ride with Dad to visit the neighborhood bars in San Francisco where he had pinball machines. He divided up the 24 bars so we made collection stops at six per week. Following Dad inside, I'd climb up on a bar stool for a Coke garnished with two maraschino cherries. Dad emptied the coin box from each machine to roll the nickels with a hand-cranked coin counter. He would consult the square board hung out of sight on the back of one pinball machine and then note something in a small book.

Just before we left, the bartender always rewarded me with a small paper bag of candy: lemon drops, candied ginger, Jordan almonds, or gum balls. I'd pass him one of the thank-you notes that Dad had put into envelopes before we left home. The notes, unbeknownst to me at the time, were for Dad's bookmaking operation rather than his pinball machines.

This ritual was interrupted only once. We were collecting at the Kezar Club on Stanyan Street. The swinging doors of the tavern opened and light cut through the dim interior. Officer Tom Sullivan, undoubtedly the biggest man I had ever seen— and no stranger to us—completely filled the door. He came over to us at the end of the bar. Dad would always buy him a drink and pass over an envelope.

"Bill, it's always a pleasure to see you." Officer Sullivan smiled at Dad while he tousled my hair. "Listen, I'm sorry but the donation has to go up. It hasn't changed in three years, so it's high time."

"What are you thinking, Tom?" Dad asked.

"Ten more a week should do."

"Tom, times are hard. I'm not making near what I used to before the Depression started. I'm sorry, but I can't donate more. Besides, if I raise you, then every other beat cop where I do any business will be expecting the same. I'm not saying you'd go out and tell them, but word would get around. You know that. I'm sorry."

"What can I say? I'm just a working stiff, and if I don't get these little contributions, I'm back to eating chuck steak. I really love having tenderloin."

"Tom, I understand. I mean we're both just trying to make a few dishonest bucks, but this is unreasonable.

"Look Bill, it's my beat. That's the new price of doing business. Take it or leave it!"

Dad went silent and stared down at his drink before turning back to the big cop.

"Listen, you greedy Irish bastard, I'll go straight before I'll pay you another dime!"

"Ah, Bill, you're embarrassing me here. Now you and your boy will have to come with me. You're under arrest for bookmaking."

Officer Sullivan let Dad lock up his truck before he placed us both in the police car he had summoned using the call-box on the corner of Stanyan and Divisidero streets.

"Take these two to the station. Bill, here, will be charged with bookmaking. Hold the boy until his mother can pick him up."

Taking the candy bag from my hand, Officer Sullivan poured the contents into his palm. He dumped the candy back on the bar and removed a wad of money from the contents of the bag. He was in no hurry, loading the candy back into the bag, then handing it to me.

"Bill, I'm ashamed of you, corrupting your son this way. If you're not careful, he could grow up to be an attorney!"

I enjoyed the police car ride and the sights and sounds of the police station better than Dad did. The officers sat me in a heavy oak chair opposite the desk sergeant and even gave me a Coke while I waited for Mom.

Dad's arrest made the news in the *San Bruno Herald*, along with a neat booking photo. I even got a mention, too. At the age of 12, I was famous—infamous, actually. Some of my friends thought my adventure was exciting, even if their moms didn't see it that way. Bea commented about it one day after school.

"My mom thinks your family is a disgrace. She thinks you must be awful."

"It was fun," I told Bea.

* * *

When I turned 12, I started working Saturdays at the Sakai flower farm. I was aware of what people called "The Depression," so I was glad to have the chance to make some money of my own and to spend time with Bea and Mr. Sakai.

They'd pick me up at my house. One morning when I opened the truck door, Mr. Sakai leaned my way. Curley had taken his usual place on Mr. Sakai's lap with his head outside the truck window as he scanning the street. The dog's long, black ears flowed out behind him, his head and one paw out the driver's window.

"Have you been arrested again?"

"No, sir."

"Okay then, you can get in," and he smiled. I liked Mr. Sakai because he was always nice to me.

We rode to the coast in silence except for sound from the radio. Bea spoke only once.

"My mother says your dad is a criminal, and you're a bad boy! She says you should be ashamed, and she wants me to play with my other friends so you don't teach me anything bad."

"I got a Coke... with two cherries." It was all I could think of to say.

Mr. Sakai drove a half-ton pickup of an uncertain vintage. It had probably once been green. The bench seat in the cab of the truck held me comfortably near the passenger window. Bea sat in the center next to her father.

Once we reached the Linda Mar area, we turned up the valley at Rockaway Beach to the Sakai field on the inland side of the coast highway. The turn was marked by a double-sided wooden sign that read "Flowers," with an arrow pointing up the packed-dirt road. The flower farm sat between the road and a small stream trailing down from the coastal mountains to the Pacific.

Arriving at the field, Mr. Sakai would unlock a small shed at the lower end by the tree-lined stream. The shed held the tools of his trade: shovels, hoes and drying racks for bulbs. In the corner, on simple wooden shelves, were larger versions of the brown glass bottles of pesticide and plant food I had seen in the garden store. Hanging from nails along the rafters were enameled lanterns Mr. Sakai used on those occasions when his work continued after sunset.

On my first Saturday at the flower field, Mr. Sakai selected a long-handled hoe for me and took a pair of light canvas gloves from a shelf.

"Pat, this is the tool you'll use. Hold it like this."

Taking the hoe, he showed me the proper way to use it. Then, handing me the gloves, he instructed me further.

"Always wear gloves so you won't get blisters on your hands. Stand up straight when you work so you don't hurt your back. Lift the hoe blade and then pull it back towards you. The curve of the blade will bite into the soil and cut off the weeds at their roots. I'm glad to see you remembered to wear a cap. This is good. Okay Pat, now you are ready to work with me...but remember, you should always check your work."

At some point I found myself noticing more about Bea than the flowers or weeds. Her hair, black and straight, was pulled back into a pony tail. Her shape, still that of a girl who had not yet begun to bloom, was unremarkable in her blue jeans and plaid flannel shirt. The details of her face, hair and her expression—especially if she smiled at me—suddenly started to matter.

"That was some long row," I said, a little louder than necessary perhaps, as I set down the hoe and stretched out my shoulders, glancing at Bea as I did. When all the drama had been milked out of the moment I turned back toward the field. My first step caught the blade of the hoe. Bang! The handle pivoted up, grazing my head with a glancing blow that pounded my ear.

"Ow!" I screamed and grabbed my ear. Then, in a rage, I picked up the hoe and pounded the ground, trying to break the offending handle.

"Pat, are you all right?" Mr. Sakai called as he walked in my direction.

Too angry to speak, I stopped my pounding only when he grabbed me from behind. One hand and forearm held my arms down while his other hand rubbed my ear.

"Breathe. The stinging will stop in a minute. Hurts, doesn't it? I did it too, once. Get yourself a drink of water from the jar in the truck, and we'll stop for lunch."

As the three of us sat by the truck, I glanced over at Bea. She avoided my eyes. My outburst had scared her.

3. Keyport, 1941

On Tuesday, December 9, the first body—that of a Spanish American War veteran—was buried in the new Golden Gate National Cemetery, according to one of the articles in the *San Bruno Herald* Mom always enclosed in her letters. I tried to picture these cemetery grounds now occupying the field I remembered from childhood, abloom in orange poppies. Dad's poem came back, too. "In Flanders fields the poppies blow, between the crosses row on row."

There was a second article clipped from the newspaper in the same envelope.

December 9, 1941

San Francisco Bay Braces for Jap Attack!

Rumors of enemy carriers off the California coast and unidentified aircraft over the Bay Area led to the closing of schools in San Francisco and Oakland. A blackout was enforced by local civil defense wardens, and local radio stations maintained radio silence from 10 a.m. until given the all-clear by the Western Defense Command at 9 p.m. Monday night.

The reports of an impending attack were deemed credible by federal authorities. Speaking from his headquarters at the Presidio, Lt. General John L. DeWitt, head of our Coast Defense District, discounted the claims by critics of a reaction based on war nerves. "Last night there were planes over this community. Enemy planes! Japanese planes! And they were tracked out to sea," stated General DeWitt.

I could smell the fear as if the newsprint had been soaked in it. It had taken only four days for Germany and Italy to declare war on us and to ally themselves with Japan.

At the end of our shift on December 14, Duano and I walked out through the main gate, headed home. Dan, our part-time postmaster, was standing on our porch.

"Nice hat," Duano said, pointing to the olive-drab World War I helmet Dan wore. A brown leather chinstrap secured the helmet to Dan's head.

Then Dan held out his right sleeve, now adorned with a green arm-band that read "Warden" in red letters. He tapped the band with his index finger. Then he tapped the front of the helmet at the crossed cannons pictured below the number 145, all stenciled in red.

"Hundred and Forty-Fifth Field Artillery, Rainbow Division."

I heard the pride in his voice as we both snapped to attention, offering crisp salutes which Dan returned, all the while shaking his head, obviously thinking we were crazy.

"So you were a cannon-cocker?" asked Duano.

"Nope, I was a cook, smart ass."

"I'm sure you were the best cook in the army. Anyway, what's up?" I asked.

"I'm the air-raid warden for the town." Dan stood more erect as he spoke. "I'm here to check on your blackout curtains." Stepping onto our porch he stared at our uncovered windows and door. "We could be next!"

"Jesus," was all we could say.

"We'll get blankets or something to cover our windows and doors," I promised. "Anyway, we're sorry and we'll get it done today," I continued, a note of contrition in my voice.

"I'll check back tonight to make sure that all your lights are out," Dan admonished as he stepped off the porch. "We don't know, but those yellow bastards could have a sub lying off the coast on the other side of the peninsula this very minute!" He shook his head as he walked. "Boy, I'd like to put my boot up the ass of every god-damn Jap in the whole god-damn Pacific." Dan spit out his angry words.

"We hear you," agreed Duano, with a nod to Dan.

Dan spoke over his shoulder as he walked away.

"One more thing. Your assigned bomb shelter, if you get caught off post during an attack, will be a slit-trench that the Rudetzsky boys are digging on the hillside, just inside the tree line." He pointed to the spot on the hillside.

"The trench will have to do until we get a proper air-raid shelter in place. The state Civil Defense guys tell me they'll be starting on it in about a week. It will be in the ground behind the store."

We stood together in silence and watched Dan walk away.

Next door at the mercantile, we found canvas tarps and nails and asked to borrow a hammer. Mrs. Olson refused our money for the tarps and nails.

"You're good boys, so I've got to keep you safe," she said, sounding more like a Mom than a landlady.

After dark that night, we ducked under the tarp covering our door so that no light would escape when the door opened. We stood together on the porch, no moon visible in the sky. The town, the station and even Seattle clear across the water had all disappeared into the night.

"It's so dark I don't think even God can see us down here tonight," said Duano.

"God probably wouldn't want to see what his world has come to," I sighed. "At least the dark is better than getting bombed, right paisano?"

"Right. We're all in the shit now, Pat."

* * *

My first post-attack contact from Bea arrived a week after Mom's letter.

December 14, 1941

Dear Pat,

I got your note about our wedding having to be put off for now. It's okay, I understand. Real or not, it seems that every white face has hardened to my family. In many San Bruno store windows there are signs now that say, "No dogs or Japs allowed." I guess we won't be shopping at Albert's Market anytime soon.

My parents put a small American flag in our front window. They've purged the house of family treasures, like their wedding pictures that showed them in traditional Japanese dress. They collected old pictures of relatives in the uniforms of Japanese military too, and Dad quietly burned it all in the back of the flower field. Dad said this was necessary so that none of our neighbors would see something that would let them imagine us to be enemy agents.

It made me sad to think of a need so great or a fear so strong that could make any family destroy the little treasures that connected them to their past. It is so hard to deal with how the white community has turned on us. My family is afraid, too. Enemy bombs can't tell our house apart from that of your parents.

We are not monsters ...we are Americans.

Love, Bea

I wanted Bea to know my feelings for her had not changed, and I was never going to be part of the problems her family now faced. I thought about things that might set me apart from the haters in her mind.

I recalled an incident back in 1938 at a San Francisco Seals baseball game. When we reached the stadium I went to buy our tickets while she stood in line to rent seat cushions.

"I'll meet you at the gate," I told her.

With tickets in hand, I walked back to the cushion line.

"Take your hand off me!" Bea shouted.

A tall white guy in a Seal's ball cap stood behind Bea with his left hand on her arm.

"Hey, keep your hands off my girl," I told him as I grabbed his shoulder, spun him around and pushed him away.

I asked Bea what happened.

"He said, 'Japs to the back of the line.' When I ignored him, he grabbed me and repeated it, just as you came back."

"So the Geisha girl is with you. Say, is it true what they say about Jap pussy?" he asked with a leer as he made a slow slanting gesture with the flat of his hand. I couldn't believe what I'd heard, so I asked him to repeat it.

"Oh, you don't know. Your Geisha isn't giving it to you? I bet you've got a needle dick, small even by Jap standards. Yeah, that's it; you're a needle dick, a button fucker!"

All the blood drained from my face and into my muscles. I punched him, the hard blows to his midsection bending him over. He fought back, landing punches of his own, but not enough to stop me. Down he went, with me on top of him, punching the whole time.

Suddenly two huge hands grabbed me, lifted and tossed me aside. Rolling onto my back, I saw the blue uniform and beefy red face of a cop. One of his large hands held a nightstick against my opponent's chest.

"You on the ground, just stay there." The tall man began to sit up, but was pushed down by the end of the nightstick. "Don't make me tell you again." The cop directed a flat stare to the man on the ground.

"You, kid, get up and go stand by the light post on the curb." I did what I was told while Bea stood beside me and we waited. The Saturday heat rolled off the cement sidewalk and stadium wall as we waited in the hot sun. We could hear crowd noise from inside and the occasional crack of a bat from the pre-game practice.

"All right, just stand there and be quiet," the cop said, adjusting his cap and putting his nightstick back into the ring on his gun belt.

"Who saw what happened?" the cop asked, looking to the small crowd that had gathered to watch the fray.

"The man on the ground was being rude to the girl," a woman said. "He tried to make her go to the end of the line because she's Japanese. Then he said something that I will not repeat," she continued, indignation apparent in her tone.

"Who else saw what happened?"

A man with two small boys answered, "It's like the woman said. The guy called her a Jap. When she wouldn't give up her place in line, he put his hand on her shoulder. The other things he said were—uh...I've got my boys here. Can I come a little closer?" The cop beckoned and the man spoke into his ear.

"Then he did this," the man added as he stepped back. He made a horizontal gesture with the flat of his hand, demonstrating what he'd seen. The cop nodded to both witnesses and advised the group to go on and enjoy the game. When the cop turned back to us, he spoke directly to Bea.

"Miss, you heard what the witnesses said, and I know about the crude remarks. Is that what happened?"

"Yes," she told him. The cop turned and looked at me for a long moment before speaking.

"Come over here for a second," he said, with a crook of two fingers. "What's your name, kid?"

When I told him, his tone changed. "Are you Bill McBride's boy?"

"Yes sir," I replied.

"I did business with your father. My name's Roy O'Donnell. Say hello to your old man for me. Now you two go on, the game is about to start. I'll take care of junior over there."

Officer O'Donnell walked back to the figure still sitting on the ground and grabbed his shoulder. "All right, asshole, get up; you're with me."

* * *

I made my letter short, but specific.

January 9, 1942
Dear Bea,

Do you remember the Saturday afternoon that we rode the bus into San Francisco for the game at Seal Stadium? I fought for you then, and I'll fight for you now. I love you and respect who you and your family are. Try not to think on the haters. Keep your focus on me and we'll make it through.

Love, Pat

We would get through these bad times and have a life together. That was what I told her in each of my letters. But weeks passed with nothing back from her. Then I heard from my mom.

February 18, 1942
Dear Son,

Dad and I are so proud that you are working for our defense industry. It's hard to know what is real or just another rumor. We are all so scared. We are under a blackout order. Dad had to paint over the headlights on his truck and the Buick. Along our coast, from the San Francisco Presidio south, the Army is setting up thousand-yard exclusion zones, which they are patrolling. Along the

23

beaches there is barbed wire on metal frames. At the first bluffs behind the beach there are big guns inside sandbag barricades. I probably shouldn't even be telling you this, but the guns are just telephone poles laid on empty cable spools facing out to sea. The poles and spools are painted gray and covered by netting that Dad says hides them from enemy planes. But there are no guns, darling. The naval base across from Tanforan has opened an induction center for recruits.

An oil tanker was torpedoed just off Santa Cruz on the north end of Monterey Bay today. Dad says that if we have to evacuate, we'll go to Uncle Warren's in Elko, Nevada. The papers say that if the Japanese invade, we can stop them at the Sierras or the Grand Canyon. Anyway, that's enough of my idle fears. I feel so bad for Bea and her family. No one has done anything nasty to them directly, but things have become very cold. The more folks get overcome with fear, the more our friends suffer. It hurts to hear Jap, Nip or Gook spoken about our friends, but everyone is so afraid. Please be careful at whatever you are doing.

Love, Mom

The papers and the radio began to bring the new reality of war ever closer with each edition and every broadcast. Mom's letter crystalized the enormity of the public's fear of invasion.

I wondered if making our defense at the Sierras or the Grand Canyon was anything more than some editor's speculation. For me, it meant somebody was ready to write off the entire West Coast, perhaps even Keyport because, in truth, we had no defenses.

Tacoma Tribune, February 23, 1942

Japs Shell Santa Barbara Oil Field

At 7 p.m. the Ellwood Oil Refinery was attacked by unknown Japanese vessels. Witnesses reported that the first rounds landed near a huge aviation fuel tank. A total of 13 shells were known to have been fired. Shells struck the Ellwood pier causing some damage, while other shots destroyed an oil derrick and a pump house.

Several local citizens reported witnessing signal lights from the unknown raider to someone on the shore.

Watching the nation's collective fear grow, it got harder for me to sound believable when writing reassurances to Bea. I was not part of the Sakai family problem, but neither was I able to be part of any solution.

Tacoma Tribune, February 24, 1942

Battle of Los Angeles!

Air raid sirens sounded at 3:16 a.m. throughout Los Angeles County when radar picked up unidentified targets 120 miles west of Los Angeles and tracked the objects to within a few miles off shore. A total blackout was ordered as coastal artillery began firing anti-aircraft shells at reported enemy aircraft. More than 1,400 shells were fired at unidentified targets with the artillery fire continuing until 4:14 a.m. when the "All Clear" was sounded. In addition to several buildings being damaged by friendly fire, three civilians were killed by falling shells and another three died of heart attacks attributed to stress from the hour-long bombardment. Sources report that Secretary of the Navy Knox described the incident as a false alarm due to "war nerves" coming on the heels of yesterday's shelling of the Ellwood Oil Refinery facility near Santa Barbara.

Prisoners of War

On February 25, 1942, the headlines in the Tacoma paper read, "President Orders Japs to be Relocated." The president had authorized the Secretary of War to create military exclusion zones. One week later, the president issued Executive Order No. 9102, which created the War Relocation Authority. By late March 1942, the presidential orders authorized "expelling all persons of Japanese ancestry, including aliens and non-aliens," from the West Coast Military Exclusion Zones. 108,000 people living in California, Washington, Oregon and Arizona were affected. No later than April 19, 1942, the military directed all Japanese people to register in person at their local post office. The order applied equally to Japanese-born naturalized citizens, American-born children of immigrants from Japan and even Koreans. The Japanese would be given a future date to report for transport to the nearest assembly center, which according to Mom, meant the Sakai family would soon be headed to Tanforan.

Mom's letters also told me about the small white satin banners being displayed in the windows of so many homes around town. A blue star meant a family member was serving in the military. A gold star signified a family member had already given their life. She'd tell me about the stars that had changed from blue to gold and the obituaries of people I knew.

In the early spring of 1942, Bea's letters described how the hardened looks coming from many were growing, along with her sense of isolation. She wasn't imagining the looks or the general hostility towards Japanese-Americans.

I understood. I wrote about how, as our fears grew, people became quick to suspect their neighbors. Having something or someone we could guard against gave people a tiny feeling of power when their world seemed to be spinning out of control.

In the face of this hardening of our society, I had no idea what I should do. Being so far away from Bea when she needed me most made my fears replay over and over in my head like a broken record.

I kept writing. I kept reassuring. These were the only tools I had at my disposal.

May 18, 1942
Dearest Pat,
On May 10, our notice was delivered to the house saying we had to report to the post office on May 15 for evacuation registration. Mom and Dad closed the store for the day and we all reported as directed. We were in line right behind the Ikedas, the Odas and the Okatas. George Okata wore his San Mateo High letterman's jacket. Dad filled out forms and we all got our pictures taken. We're supposed to receive special photo ID badges to wear when we report for relocation.

I suppose it could have been worse; it could have been arm bands like the Nazis make the Jews wear. I suppose ours would have a red rising sun instead of a yellow Star of David. Our report date will be in September, but that was all we were told, except we are to report to Tanforan. After the pictures, we moved on to vaccinations. We each got two

They said we were being vaccinated against communicable diseases as a public health measure. Some of the children were scared of the shots and cried. Little Robert Oda was in front of me in line. He didn't speak or cry, but passed out when the nurse gave him the first injection. I helped his mom get him up, and I don't think he even knew he got the second shot. With my I.D. picture and shots, I felt like all I was missing was an ear tag by the end of this cattle call.

Work at the bank has changed, too. The other tellers who have been my friends are still polite, but polite is different than friendly. Thankfully, Betty and Janet haven't changed, so I don't feel totally alone, but I notice the difference. Customers move from my line to use other windows if they think I'm not looking, but I always notice. Mr. Weber, the branch manager, took me aside and told me my job with Bank of America was safe, and I need not worry. He was trying to be nice, but it really didn't help. They're lucky to have already changed the name from Bank of Italy to B of A, or they'd probably be losing customers.

I don't know what all this means for us, my love. On my lunch hour, I walked from the bank up El Camino to Tanforan. All the beautiful flowers in the infield are gone. The infield, stables and parking areas are all being turned into rows of low wood buildings. I guess this is part of the ugly change: racetrack to assembly center. Here we all are, racing to war.

Anyway, I'm fine. Work helps me not miss you so much. I'm trying very hard not to hate them all back.

Love, Bea

Reading Bea's letter made my throat thicken with emotion, and it made me mad at my government. I got up from the table and spit into the sink. A drink of water eased the lump in my throat. Then my fist slammed down on my glass, which shattered, cutting my palm and little finger.

"Son of a bitch," I growled, as my hand throbbed and blood flowed onto the drain board. I grabbed a dishtowel from the oven door and wrapped up my bleeding hand.

I hated the Empire of Japan, while at the same time hating what my own government was doing to my Japanese-American friends. I knew Bea and her family were not the "yellow peril" that the papers and the movies were selling.

Having my heart in one place and my body in another was getting harder and harder by the day. The bad news in her letters was paralleled by bad news from the war. In April and May of 1942, small forest fires were started along the Oregon coast by incendiary bombs carried on balloons launched from Japanese submarines. Two hikers were killed when they accidently picked up one of the devices that had not gone off.

Our precious aircraft carriers were being lost. The *Lexington* was sunk in May during the Battle of the Coral Sea, and the *Yorktown* was lost in June at the Battle of Midway. In June of 1942, eight German agents were caught on the New Jersey shore after landing by submarine. France fell to the Germans. Attu in the Aleutian Islands was invaded by Japanese marines. We lost the *Wasp* in September off Guadalcanal and the *Hornet* in October during the Battle of the Santa Cruz Islands.

* * *

"Duano, if they do come, what do you want to do?" We'd volunteered for the Auxiliary Defense Force at the earliest opportunity and each of us was issued a World War I, bolt-action Springfield rifle, an old-style steel helmet and 50 rounds of ammunition.

"The Japs are not kind to prisoners. They think it's shameful to surrender. I believe the stories from the Philippines and what they did to the Australians they captured. I say we fight if we can." Duano's voice had no hint of boasting as he matter-of-factly pronounced his plan.

"If it comes to that, I'm with you. We'll fight where we stand. Then when we've kicked the shit out of 'em, we'll have a beer, right?"

4.   Pacifica, California, 1934

A mile up the Linda Mar Valley, beyond the Sakai flower field, was a trout farm. The small, square artificial pond was hidden on three sides by tall trees and an understory of shrubs. "Suicide fish," is what Mr. Sakai called the captives of the pond.

The trout farm provided fishing gear along with a one-gallon galvanized bucket for our catch and a paper cup with the liver cubes for bait. The fish, all hatchery raised, were a uniform eight to ten inches long, and silver with just a hint of their namesake rainbow color. On our first trip to the trout farm, Mr. Sakai gave us one of what would be several fishing lessons.

"Okay, you two," he said, as he knelt on one knee. He took a single cube of raw, red liver from the paper bait cup. He held it in one hand, between thumb and forefinger, with my fish hook in his other hand.

"Watch how I put the hook through the bait but keep its sharp point exposed? You have to leave the tip of the hook out to catch the fish. Otherwise, if the point is covered, the fish will chew the bait off without getting hooked. Always check your work. Do you see?"

We both nodded.

"Okay, now each of you try it," he told us.

Finally, after several clumsy attempts, one which included spilling the bait cup and nearly losing the pole and reel in the pond, Bea and I managed to bait our own hooks.

"Like this?" I asked, holding out my baited hook for his inspection.

"Very good" His praise was accompanied by two nods, then he began his next tutorial.

"Now, here is how you cast your line into the water. It takes practice, so don't worry about trying to cast clear out into the middle of the pond. The fish swim all around so they'll find your bait no matter where you end up."

There would be more practicing and missteps as I stood by Bea at the edge of the pond. Finally, our baited hooks managed to make it out into the water under our own power.

"Very nice. Now, the last thing to remember is to keep the tip of your rods up."

Reaching over to the pole I was clutching in a death grip with both hands, Mr. Sakai gently lifted under the heel of my hands, adjusting my grip.

"Like that, Pat, just keep the tip up. Now, when the fish bites, remember to keep the rod tip up as you crank in the line so the fish can't get away. Okay, you can catch two fish for each person in your family." He was a patient teacher who encouraged more than he corrected.

One cast and one fish was always how it worked. This was not a game of skill, but rather a well-organized harvest.

"Do you want me to help you get your last two fish?" I asked Bea one Saturday afternoon. A confirming nod came from my companion.

Our lines went back into the water at the same time. A fish hit Bea's bait just a few seconds before the tip of my pole also jerked, signaling the arrival of our final fish of the day. Reeling our fish to the surface, we hoisted them out of the water and lowered our rods to get the two flopping fish onto the bare packed dirt. Bea's fish had swallowed the hook and it flopped around her feet until her dad, abandoning the shade of a tree, came over to help separate fish from the line and put it in our bucket. Wiggling and somersaulting in the air, my fish— now free from the hook—bounced on the dirt and in two reflexive flops, fell over the bank and down the slope toward the creek that flowed behind the trout farm. I bounded down the bank myself, following the flopping fish until it stopped in the alders that lined the creek. Fish in hand, I turned to find Bea right beside me. The air was cool in the shade of the alder trees along the creek. Ferns lined the creek banks as the clear water glittered in the filtered sun.

Leaning forward, I planted a quick kiss on her cheek. Bea's eyes opened wider in surprise, but then she smiled. With a solemn expression on her face, she reached out with one finger and traced down the silver side of the trout and then rubbed the tip of my nose. Nothing was said, and the only sound came from the creek. The she quickly leaned over, kissed my cheek and ran up the bank back to the pond.

5.   San Bruno, 1934

One evening when I was 13, Bea and I were studying at the desk in her room. Her door remained open, a required propriety and a sign of respect to her parents.

"I better head home," I told her.

"Yes, it's after seven, and I've had enough world history for one day."

"Can I use your bathroom before I leave?"

"Sure. You know where it is," Bea replied without looking up from her book. As I passed the door to her brother's room, I heard the three-quarter time sound of "Blue Moon", from the new movie, *Manhattan Melodrama*. Curley, hearing movement in the hallway, appeared from the front room and met me at the bathroom door. I went to one knee long enough to give him a quick scratch behind one of his dangling ears.

I closed the bathroom door. Through the open window high on the wall to my left, I heard Bea's parents from the adjoining kitchen, which also must have had a window open to the evening air. I may not have understood everything, but I remembered it all just the same.

"Oishi, our daughter has bloomed."

"You mean?"

"Yes, she bleeds. I've kept quiet about her and the boy. Their friendship was harmless until now. We must start shaping her future, as ours was shaped for us by our parents back in Japan. I'll start looking for a suitable Japanese family with a son. I know what to do, husband."

"Taeko, my vision of the future is perhaps broader than yours. The boy is a good fit for her. He is right for this time and place. I understand your mind is rooted in our home culture, but where you may see problems, I can see promise in this match.

The world is changing. It is changing more than you know, more than I can say. You will trust me on this!"

"Oishi, don't be a fool! Our daughter can't be matched to a white devil. I can't bear the shame of her marrying an unclean white. I'd rather she marry one of those stinking garlic-eating Koreans than a white! This cannot be. She must become Japanese."

"Taeko, you forget your place and your duty. I will not discourage them and neither will you! Do you understand me?" Mr. Sakai's voice rose as he uttered the command.

"Yes, husband," was her only reply.

I imagined her head bowed and her eyes downcast. The response was spoken in barely more than a whisper. I heard Mr. Sakai leaving the kitchen, and then Mrs. Sakai hissed her final words under her breath.

"In a pig's ass, husband. I'll not let my daughter be corrupted by a white devil with dirty hands."

* * *

San Mateo, California, had a thriving Japan Town and Mrs. Sakai decided that picking a boy from that community would be easy enough to conceal in the fabric of her daily life. Mrs. Sakai was strong in her traditional beliefs about raising a daughter. She planned to guide by using an unseen hand, gently pushing Bea into the Japanese community and to a Japanese future. Her duty to her husband would always appear served, while only a thin coat of marital lacquer covered her own plans.

She would make herself my greatest obstacle to ever having a future with Bea. I would never overcome the pressure of her unseen hand guiding her daughter's future.

* * *

Sumi Shimizono, or Rose, as she was known by her white customers, owned the largest market in San Mateo. Purity Market was a community hub for all things Japanese. Mr. Shimizono stocked the store with goods his import business brought from the home islands. Japanese imports arrived in San Francisco, and Shimizono-owned trucks brought the items to the Shimizono warehouse. From there, goods were disbursed to the four Purity Markets that trailed south along the El Camino Real between San Mateo and San Jose.

Taeko Sakai bought nursery stock from the Shimizono Company and, in turn, sold them cut flowers. These long-established links played well into the plan of Mrs. Sakai's stealthy match-making. Russell Shimizono, two years older than Beatrice, would do as husband material—if the match also seemed to serve the Shimizono family.

Monday morning at eight was Takeo's regular trip to Shimizono's. The exchange of goods complete, she leaned over the counter and spoke to Mrs. Shimizono, addressing her by her Japanese name.

"Sumi, can you pause for tea? I have an important matter to discuss."

The request was spoken in Japanese, signifying the privacy and importance of the topic. Sumi Shimizono smiled and nodded.

"Let me finish this order, and I'll meet you at a table in the front of the market."

Taeko Sakai chose a table by the window. She ordered tea and rice cookies, which arrived as Sumi sat down. Tea was poured and sipped before a word was spoken.

"My daughter has arrived as a young lady."

"I understand," offered Sumi, speaking delicately over the rim of her tea cup.

"It is time for me to help her become the good Japanese woman that is expected. For too long now she has been schooling, playing and working with young whites. She knows no better. Now it is time for me to gently bend her to her proper future. She deserves to be shaped into a good Japanese wife, even if she doesn't know it. She has not yet been corrupted by whites, but the turn of events requires me to act now."

Sumi leaned into the table. "I understand. You were like me. Our marriages were arranged for us back home in Japan. I thank my parents for making me the wife I am today. My husband, Hiro, was a good match. I only hope Russell and Beatrice will find good mates. You are a good mother, Taeko."

"I wanted to propose that we match Russell and Beatrice. Would you consider such a match, Sumi? I think our children would be a good fit. What do you think?"

"And your husband, does he feels the same?"

"No, the stupid man doesn't see the danger. He talks about duty and his visions of the future. Oishi thinks a mere woman cannot understand. He ordered me not to interfere with the child's silly games. Intentionally or not, he allows her too much contact with their world. So you understand. I must perform my duty to arrange a suitable marriage while hiding my work in plain sight."

"Oh yes, my husband is like that, too. He puffs up and tries to tell me what I can and cannot do. Fortunately, they are all just big, horny boys, aren't they?" Sumi said with a shy smile. "Give me two weeks to consider your proposal. You and I understand; wherever we live, we will always be Japanese. Why men can't see this, I'll never comprehend."

Two weeks later, over the same table where the negotiation had begun, the mothers struck a deal. They would quietly guide their children toward a shared path so when Russell and Beatrice finally were one, the young man and woman would look back and think it had been their own idea.

6.   San Bruno, 1934

When Mr. Sakai pulled up to our curb, Curley's head poked out of the driver's side window. His pink tongue hung out of his mouth as he panted, dog drool dripping onto the truck's door. Bea was not sitting next to her father. I got into the truck and pulled the door closed to the customary squeal of rusty hinges

"Turn toward me," Mr. Sakai directed. "Tell me about your cheek."

My cheek was quite plainly bruised. I faced him across the cab of the truck.

"There's this seventh grader, Curt. He's been taking my lunch money."

"Did you tell your father about this?"

"Dad said I should stand up for myself. I tried, but he's bigger than I am. "

"Ah, I see," and then he paused for a moment before continuing. "I will teach you how to defend yourself," he said. "If your enemy is bigger, then what you must do is strike first. Don't be noble and wait to be hit. You will lose your advantage. Strike hard when he isn't expecting it, and you won't be bullied anymore."

"Yes, sir, but he'll hurt me."

"Believe me, Patrick, it will work. I'll show you where to hit him when we get to the field. You'll be fine."

"Where's Bea?"

"Her mother has her making deliveries for the shop today. She says hello, and she'll see you at school on Monday."

I think Mr. Sakai read the disappointment in my face. His right hand patted my shoulder. I was seeing less and less of Bea as time went by.

"Her mother needs her for the shop and to help with deliveries to Shimozono's, our biggest customer. Their son,

Russell, is a junior at San Mateo High school with you and my daughter. Has she ever mentioned him?" She hadn't mentioned him, but I knew of Russell. He was star of the tennis team.

Mrs. Sakai found reasons to send Bea by bus to the Shimizono store several times a week. Later, Bea recalled for me how her mother had contrived to bring her into the Shimizono orbit.

"I need you to deliver this special order of flowers to Mrs. Shimizono."

Some mornings over breakfast the needs of the family business were announced.

"Bea, Ernie has football practice after school, so please come right home and help me get these blooms to San Mateo."

Often the directions were summarized in a simple phrase, "I'll be needing your help all week."

Unknown to me was that Russell Shimizono usually met her in San Mateo. Russell was polite and formal in small ways uncommon in the working class boys of San Bruno like me. His hands were always clean, and he seemed to have an unlimited supply of ironed khaki trousers.

"May I treat us to a soda at the store before you head home?"

Sometimes the offer was for a ride home in one of the company trucks, rather than a return bus or train ride. Extending a clean hand to Bea he assisted her into the delivery truck.

"This is much nicer than a bus ride home, don't you think?"

7.   San Bruno, 1935

On May 30, Decoration Day, the poppies came out across the nation. Dad belonged to the local VFW post and took his turn selling the glossy red paper flowers. The VFW flowers reminded me of the poem about the poppies in Flanders fields.

Pinned to his shirt pocket was the one service medal he kept in a small silver box. Dad had won the box in a poker game from Johnny McCrae, a Canadian doctor. Dad's World War I Victory Medal, a round brass medallion, hung beneath the one and one-half inch of tri-colored ribbon. Bisecting the ribbon, a single campaign bar showed "France" in raised letters.

Sitting in a corner of our living room were three brass 75mm artillery shell casings. Two were ornate, patterned with roses, the symbol of the Argonne. Dad had traded cigarettes to German prisoners of war for the casings. The decorating of shell casing, done by hand using wooden tools, provided their only source of exchange for what small comforts could be had. The third shell casing, plain and crude in its adornment, bore only three capital letters, AEF, for Allied Expeditionary Force. "I did that one myself, using the tines of a fork and the handle of my bayonet for a hammer," Dad had explained to me years ago.

After Dad's two-hour shift selling poppies, he met Mom and me where we waited on the sidewalk along the route of the annual Posey Parade in downtown San Bruno. There were high school bands, color guard units from each of the armed services, and the Shriners on bikes, their fez tassels whipping their faces. Marching groups of women in large hats alternated with homemade floats decorated with thousands of paper flowers. Across the street, I saw Mr. and Mrs. Sakai and Curley next to another Japanese family. I assumed they were the parents of Russell, the boy who had been spending so much time with Bea. Russell and Bea were to be riding a Shimizono-sponsored float celebrating the beauty of local spring flowers.

The Shimizono float came into view. Bea and Russell stood together under a glistening white lath arch trimmed in red carnations. Their pose reminded me of the ceramic figures on top of a wedding cake. Fresh carnations of vivid reds, whites and whites dyed to a soft blue had been woven into the shape of American flags on both sides of the float.

Bea was dressed in a pink gown and had pink flowers crowning her hair. She smiled at the crowd and gave a slow prom-queen wave: elbow-elbow, wrist-wrist. Russell was dressed in white slacks and a white V-neck sweater, trimmed in red and blue. He tossed cellophane-wrapped hard candy to children as the float rolled along. Bea smiled happily at her own family, and then turned to smile at my family.

Two older teens pushed away from the crowd and into the street. I recognized them, the Craig twins, Curt and Burt. Each carried a covered steel lunch bucket, and they fell in line behind the Shimizono float. With a nod to each other, the two opened the buckets and began throwing fish heads at Bea and Russell. An invisible blanket of rotted fish smell leapt out of the two lunch buckets and wafted in all directions. The first fish head hit Bea in the middle of her back. A hemorrhage of fish scales appeared on her gown. She screamed in surprise and turned to see what had struck her, just as two more fish heads splattered her dress and bare shoulder.

"Stop it!" she screamed at the attackers.

"Japs go home! Japs go home!" the two teens shouted back.

Mrs. Sakai gasped, and Mrs. Shimizono fainted dramatically, falling into the arms of her fat husband. Russell took several hits in quick succession, and then stepped outside of the lath arch, using it to shield himself from the fish-head missiles. Bea, now standing in the arch alone, faced her attackers head-on, screaming, "Stop it!"

I ran from the curb into the street just as Mr. Sakai ran in from the opposite curb. Then Curley joined the fray. Mr. Sakai grabbed the nearest attacker in a bear hug, lifting the teen off his feet and throwing him to the ground, then resting his foot on the offender's neck. Curley clamped his jaws on the attacker's ankle. Running full-tilt, I hit Curt Craig, knocking the bucket from his hands. Down he went, face first on the asphalt. On his back now, I hit him with my fists, roundhouse after roundhouse punches to his head and torso.

"You son-of-a-bitch, I'll kill you!"

I kept punching until my dad pulled me off and secured the teen to the street by putting a boot on his chest. I ran over and hopped up on the float. Still shaking from adrenalin, I grabbed Bea and pulled her to me, wrapping both arms around her.

"Are you all right?"

Bea could only nod, her chin bent softly into the flesh of my neck.

Looking over at Russell, I asked if he was all right. He was still hanging on to the arch for dear life, using it for cover, even though both attackers were safely on the ground.

"Yes, thank you," he responded in a weak and rattled voice.

Mr. Shimizono came over and stood next to the soiled float. He motioned Russell down, and held him at arm's length with one hand while holding his nose with the other as they walked back towards his wife. Mrs. Sakai stood at Mrs. Shimizono's side, her eyes downcast.

Two city cops arrived and took the attackers away, to the hearty cheers of spectators and parade participants both. Bea's father climbed onto the float. His arms encircled us both.

"I'll take her home now. Thank you, Pat."

Stepping back and releasing Bea from my arms, I saw that my fists had scraped the asphalt when I had thrown punches at Curt Craig. The fish stains and stink on Bea's dress were now mixed with bloodstains from my hands. I climbed down and walked to the curb. Mom pulled a handkerchief from her purse and wrapped it around one of my hands and I pushed the other fist into it, hoping to stop the bleeding.

The parade regained its form and marched on around the stopped float. As the three families began to move apart, I looked back over my shoulder towards Bea. Her father still held her close. I saw him turn to his wife, and heard one simple word passed between them.

"Enough!"

* * *

On Saturday morning after the Posey Parade attack, Mr. Sakai pulled up in front of my house. Curley's head was halfway out of the driver's side window as he sat on Mr. Sakai's lap. Seeing me, he backed himself out of the window. Bea was seated next to her dad. Curley pivoted across her lap, presenting himself to me for an acknowledging scratch behind his ear. She held my hand for the ride to the coast, but nothing was said. When we got out next to the field of blooming flowers, her dad walked off to get tools. We stood by the truck.

"You're awful. Not like Russell," she said.

I didn't know what to think or say for a moment, until my reprieve came in the form of her smile and a hug, as she briefly rested her head on my shoulder. Bea took my hands up from my sides. She looked at the healing wounds and softly kissed each knuckle.

"Thank you," was all she said.

* * *

Now 15, we no longer just pulled suicide fish from the trout farm, but harvested from the ocean as well. The south end of Rockaway Beach ended at the sharply rising cliffs of Pedro Point. The rock bluff of the point yielded to a small roadway on the ocean side. A single dirt lane ran to Hidden Cove. Nestled in a protected niche south of Pedro Point, the cove lived up to its exotic name by virtue of the difficult access.

Leading us down to the beach, Mr. Sakai showed us the blue-black mussels that covered every inch of the jagged rocks guarding the mouth of the cove. The coarse brown sand of the beach could only be walked at low tide. If the tide was out, we would stop at the cove after our work in the flower field instead of going to the trout farm.

At 15, Bea's flannel work clothes now fit her differently. The wind in her face, her hair blowing and her shirt pressed against her torso as we worked side-by-side, showed off her gentle new curves. Unspoken, we fell into a pattern. We walked hand in hand now when we were alone in the cove. When we finished gathering our mussels, we would sit on the rocks by her dad's truck and take turns drying each other's feet.

* * *

Back home in San Bruno at our first mussel dinner, my dad asked where we had gathered the mollusks. The steaming pot of sea food filled the kitchen with the smells of seaweed and salt air.

"Hidden Cove, around past Pedro Point?"

When Mom was out of the room, he leaned over to my seat at the table. It was an open secret in our house that Dad had his finger in many illegal pies, though he described them as "public service businesses." Dad had given up bootlegging when Prohibition ended in 1933.

"That's where we used to bring in the alcohol for my gin."

My dad, always suspicious of "the Bible thumping church ladies," had passed along the basics of making and marketing bathtub hooch. This qualified as fatherly advice in Dad's mind.

"You see my boy, when the Prohibition started the people who made liquor bottles or printed liquor labels were still in business. So what you wanted to do was convince your customers you were selling the real goods that you'd smuggled down from Canada. My brand was Gordon's Gin. I had the same embossed bottles and multi-colored labels. Except for the federal tax stamp seal, my product looked genuine. Nobody knew I had mixed it up in a steel beer keg in the back of our garage.

In some parts of town, there still were illegal slot machines for the back rooms of his customers, as well as pinball machines for the front areas of their bars. My dad was dangerous in ways the hard-working, steady and uncomplicated Mr. Sakai was not. They were so different—one an honest family man and the other something else entirely. It would take me almost 50 years to understand how, just like the tide line on its rock, Hidden Cove had left its mark on both of these men.

8.   San Bruno, 1936

It was after 10th grade I started telling my family I wanted to be a railroad man. Graduating from high school was good, but a job was essential. Bea was the first to hear my dream.

Walking downtown with Curley leading the way, we stopped for ice cream cones at Shaw's. I had frozen strawberry while Bea chose rocky road. Curley, as usual, got a scoop of vanilla served in a cup. Propelled by Curley's tongue, the ice cream cup skittered around our feet until I knelt down and held it still. He took the frozen treat in bites, not seeming to bothering with any taste until his pink tongue had scoured the last bit from the cup. Then he sat down at our feet and rolled his eyes in delight before shifting a fixed gaze to our cones, hoping we would share.

"I've been giving a lot of thought to the future," I said. "It's not that I hate school. I know I need reading, writing and math, but I've gotten all that now. I'm not so sure the other stuff, like history, biology or gym class, is ever going to help me get a job. Here's my plan. I want to get a job with the railroad. It would be an adventure and something I could be good at."

"The railroad?" Bea seemed puzzled, so I explained my dream.

"Dad's two brothers, my uncles Warren and Gerald, are railroad men. Uncle Warren wears these Ben Davis bib overalls—with gray and white stripes—and a long-sleeve shirt. He's as tough as the smiling gorilla logo on his clothes. The gorilla logo reminds me of the comic strip 'Alley Oop,' the one that's just above my favorite, 'Pogo,' in the Sunday funnies." I had her full attention now and she smiled.

"Go on."

"Anyway, when I was six, Mom took me to visit Uncle Warren and Aunt Luella in Elko, Nevada. Uncle Warren let me drive a locomotive a couple of feet in the rail yard.

"If that is what you love, then that's what you should try for," Bea said as she returned my smile. Bea was strong enough not to be led, but she made no attempt to control me. I liked that she supported what I wanted.

I asked my dad and wrote my uncles to see if they knew anyone at the San Francisco yard. All three told me the man to see was the yardmaster, Dallas Long. Dad knew Mr. Long from the Log Cabin Bar, one of his spots that Mr. Long frequented. Uncle Warren and Uncle Gerald knew him through the railroad.

At age 16, I met Mr. Long at the Southern Pacific yard in San Francisco. I was primed by both my uncles for the meeting. My answers to his questions all consisted of "Yes sir," or "No sir." Mr. Long's slow Texas drawl and his imposing height only added to his larger-than-life position in my mind and in my future.

"I want to be a railroad man, sir. High school is fine, but I wouldn't be there if I didn't have to be. I'd like to be here if I could."

An apprenticeship offer came two months later.

The first day of my apprenticeship was November 18, 1936. Dad dropped me off on his way to work. Stopping in front of the rail yard office, Dad pointed to a single galvanized post. At the top was a small metal sign reading, "Bus Stop," superimposed over the embossed figure of a running greyhound dog.

"That's how you get home tonight and to work tomorrow," he said.

My apprenticeship had no preset length, unlike the clearly defined high school years. You were an apprentice until you could do the job. It was that simple. The smells of machine oil in the shop and the sharp odor of creosote from the rail yard became familiar. I learned the machine shop from the ground up. Long before being allowed to touch a machine, I swept floors and carried buckets of metal shavings from beneath the lathes and grinders. My hands got dirty doing whatever I was told to do.

In the fall of 1938, Mr. Long called me away from my work one afternoon.

"Pat, the shop foreman tells me your work is journeyman quality now. He and I agree that you're not an apprentice anymore, so now you'll be receiving journeyman pay."

When I told Bea the good news, she beamed a smile and told me she was proud but not surprised. Then she glanced around before planting a kiss on my cheek.

After mastering the lathe and drill press, I chose to reach for the heights by conquering the grinder. Using a grinder was a blend of art and skill. Grinding metal meant gauging depths correctly by both eye and feel. A successful grinder had to "be one" with the grinding disk, even before checking his work with the most delicate tools. The grinder took all of the skills I had learned as mere starting points to build on. Like a sculptor who can see the finished statue inside the uncarved block, the grinder sees and feels how much metal to remove to free up the machine part inside.

Gradually, I changed—on both the inside and the outside. Oxford shoes became steel-toed boots. Jeans and my ever-present two-tone wind breaker became Ben Davis overalls, shirt and jacket, all bearing the smiling gorilla logo. Planning ahead and double-checking my work became second nature to me. Many of the small lessons I had received from Mr. Sakai, my patient teacher, helped me now.

I could still his voice inside my head. "Always check your work."

9.   San Francisco, 1940

In late 1939, the Bureau of Ordnance, part of our War Department, began to advertise for machinists.

Machinists and Engineers needed for defense work!
Excellent pay if you meet our standards.
Call Templebar 8-2014, or visit the Federal Building,
450 Golden Gate, San Francisco, Room 301.
Help keep us strong and ready!

The talk over beers after work at the rail yard was about how the pay would be 50 percent higher than at the railroad. Even more seductive was how the jobs included the new concepts of paid medical care and a retirement after 20 years of government work. The following day I asked my boss for a morning off, which he approved and scheduled for the next Monday.

I rode to the city with my dad and went to the Federal Building. Inside Room 301, rows of chairs faced a dark wood counter. The room was filled with applicants and in turn the air filled with the sharp smells of nervous bodies and Bay Rum cologne. Forty minutes after my completed application had gone into the appropriate box, I saw it being put on the desk at an interview station. The form was picked up by a man in a brown suit, white shirt and a tie. He walked over to the counter that separated the applicants from the interviewers. His sleeves were rolled up and the suit jacket hung over the back of his desk chair.

"Patrick McBride," he called.

I followed him back to his desk and took a seat. The application was short: two pages double-sided. Questions about school, work history, residences and family filled the four sides of the form. When the interviewer spoke, his questions were a bit of a letdown.

"Well, I can read your writing, so you've made a good start. We'll verify your work history and if you qualify, we'll let you know. Are you willing to go wherever your country needs you?"

"Absolutely"

"Thanks for coming in today," he said, as he stood and offered me a handshake over the desk.

In the weeks to come I heard about how "men in suits" had spoken to the railroad company personnel office, my shop foreman and our neighbors in San Bruno.

In February 1940, I was offered a machinist job at Keyport, Washington.

I had to report to the Commander, Naval Torpedo Station at Keyport, in just two weeks. I would get travel pay of $10 per day from San Bruno to Keyport and a train ticket. My starting pay would be 50 percent higher than my railroad job and there were opportunities for overtime. Plus, the letter went on.

If you are now subject to the provisions of the Selective Service Act, Bureau of Ordnance employment exempts you from the military draft during the time you shall maintain this essential work.

Mom was standing at the sink and Dad was sitting at our kitchen table finishing a sandwich and a beer.

"I got the job," I shouted and waved the letter.

My folks continued to look at me silently, a proud smile on Dad's face and a more worried look on Mom's as they took turns reading the letter.

"Your Uncle Burt is up in Seattle, so maybe he could meet you at the train and put you up until you get settled. Just so you know, he's a cheap bastard. In fact, he's so cheap he'd steal the nickels off a dead nigger's eyes, so he might want to charge you rent. But if you like, I'll call Burt and see if he can help out until you start work."

"Oh, Bill!" muttered Mom, shaking her head. I was not shocked at all. This was just my dad, a man of his age who, without thought or animosity, spoke of "coons, wops, kikes, spicks, chinks, krauts," and sometimes even "japs."

"Okay, Dad. Go ahead and ask Uncle Burt if he can meet me and put me up when I arrive in Seattle."

I remembered being mad at Uncle Burt. He had convinced me the Straits of Juan de Fuca were named after the governor's wife, Wanda Fuca.

Telling that story as part of my report describing my summer vacation in front of Miss Wren's fifth-grade class had gotten me a gentle but public correction from the teacher. Burt had made me look foolish when I was trying to look smart. I was now finally old enough to forgive him and appreciate his humor.

In the background, the radio played a new instrumental version of Rogers and Hart's song, "Blue Moon." The familiar lyrics came automatically into my head. I remembered that "Blue Moon" had probably been the last song John Dillinger heard before he walked out of the Biograph Theater and was gunned down on the street.

* * *

With only two weeks before my reporting date at Keyport, there was much to do. I called the train station and found that the trip up would take two days. I figured on another day at the Washington end for arrival and getting to Keyport. This left me part of the 11 remaining days to give notice at work, pack, and see family and friends. Tonight...tonight, I would ask Bea to marry me.

* * *

I secured the use of my parents' Buick, then called and asked Bea if she could go out that night.

"It's important, I have big news."

An hour later, I was on the Sakai's front porch, waiting under the amber glow of the porch light. Mrs. Sakai, who never spoke to me, answered my knock at the door, Curley at her feet. I knelt and gave him my usual scratch-behind-the-ear greeting while I waited in the entry hall for Bea to appear. Relaxing under the touch of my greeting, the dog farted loudly, turning his head away as he did, as if to communicate, "Wasn't me."

"Curley," I said, hastening to my feet and facing Mr. Sakai, who was seated across their front room. I squared my shoulders and spoke my news to Bea's father.

"I got the job I wanted. It's double the pay I'm getting now. And I won't be drafted! I'm going to the torpedo works at Keyport, Washington, in two weeks."

Ernie paused from his homework to toss his congratulations in my direction. Mr. Sakai, rising from his chair, came over and shook my hand. Mrs. Sakai didn't acknowledge my news and instead walked off into the kitchen.

"Pat, I'm proud of you. I want to hear all the details, but not tonight. You've got a movie to go see."

Bea appeared at the far end of the hallway. She had on her favorite poodle skirt and a pink angora sweater. Flashing a quick finger to my lips to Mr. Sakai and Ernie, I turned to smile at her.

"I've got news! I'll tell you in the car."

We parked in the front row of the drive-in, both for privacy and to hopefully see through the fog that dimmed even the 50-foot-high screen. Parked now, I turned smiling, and took her hand.

"I got a machinist job with the government, Bea. They want me to be in Washington State in just two weeks."

Bea listened silently.

"I'll be exempt from the draft too. I know it's not perfect, because I'll be away, but this will make our future."

"It seems so far away..." said Bea. A long pause, and an exaggerated pout came to her lips as she he turned to me, "Do you think you'll find a new girlfriend up there?"

Her question shocked me. Was she serious? Was she having doubts about me or about us?

"Only if you won't wait for me. Bea, I love you. I want to marry you. I've wanted to marry you since we were sixteen, but I needed to get a job and establish myself before I could ask. I can only give my innocence once, and I want to give it to you, when you're ready. Like you always told me, you are worth waiting for. Wait for me now, just until we know the job is going to work out. Then marry me and you can move there. We'll find a bank up there that needs a smart and beautiful teller."

I knew that legally I wasn't supposed to marry outside my race. I didn't care. I'd find a way, or like my father, illegality would become one part of my life. Bea snuggled closer and her responses to my declaration were smiles and kisses, interspersed between questions, before she added the most important response.

"I do love you, too. Yes, my love. I knew I'd marry you, ever since you saved me at the Posey Parade. You fought for me when Russell only thought to save himself. Oh yes, I'll marry you."

Bea's words washed over me, causing my skin to tingle. Warmed by our breath and body heat, the car windows fogged up. What happened next was fast, quiet and unforgettable.

"I want to be your first too. I'm afraid though. I can't get pregnant. What can we do?"

"I'll stop before I finish, I promise."

"Are you sure you can?"

"Yes."

We each made the quick necessary preparations. Belt unbuckled, trousers opened and pulled down behind my thighs, and undershorts wiggled down. Bea slipped her white underpants off from beneath her skirt. She climbed onto my lap, her back braced by the bottom edge of the steering wheel, careful to avoid leaning on the horn. We joined, warm and wet, moving into each other in slow rhythm. My arms were around her, holding her sides. I kissed her face and lips, my eyes closed. I listened to her breathing and concentrated on my own sensations, my promise to withdraw hanging heavy in my mind.

"I have to stop." I felt the uncontrollable rush beginning deep in my groin.

We each quickly rolled our hips away from our joining. I grabbed the handkerchief I had placed next to me on the seat and covered my erection, finishing seconds later. We dressed quickly before entwining once again.

Our hugs and kisses were tender, softer, yet somehow more passionate than before. Tonight for us was an act of commitment. In the afterglow of our love, I realized the enormity of the gift Bea had just given me. The willing gift of her virginity, not lightly given and never reclaimable, showed me that Bea had chosen me for her life mate—deliberately, as I had chosen her.

"Thank you. I was afraid that you might give me a kiss on the cheek and wish me good luck. Instead you gave me yourself. I don't want anything or anyone else, ever. God, I love you so."

Silently, I held her tight.

"We'd better go. The movie's over," Bea said softly after some time had passed.

The fog cleared slightly as we neared San Bruno. The parking lot of the El Camino drive-in diner backed on to the rear of the Sakai garden store. We took seats in a green and gold upholstered booth, ordered Cokes and burgers. Then we excused ourselves to the adjoining restrooms.

Standing at the urinal, I glanced down and was shocked at the blood on my penis and the white of my Jockey shorts. I dampened paper towels and moved to the toilet stall, latching the door behind me. My crotch and upper thighs were smeared with dried blood. I cleaned myself up and returned to the sink to wash my hands before leaving the restroom. I met Bea as she emerged from the ladies' room.

"Are you all right? There was blood. Did I do something wrong? Did I hurt you?"

"No, I'm fine," she replied, taking my hand in hers. "There's always blood the first time."

I squeezed her hand, relieved that the biggest moment of my life had not been a disaster after all. We ate and talked about my new job, our imagined future, and how hard it would be to leave the homes and friends we had grown up with.

"Let's don't tell anyone yet, so our secret is safe until you know we are going to be okay at Keyport," cautioned Bea.

* * *

The next days were filled with the newness of our secrets. We were lovers and going to get married. On our last remaining weekend, we drove to Stockton so I could meet her cousin, Margie Watanabe. The Watanabe family had a walnut orchard and a small truck garden. When we arrived, Bea and Margie walked off hand in hand, speaking in hushed tones. When they returned a few moments later, their private conversation ended. We all walked together under the big walnut tree in the Watanabe's front yard towards the shade of their covered porch—Bea at my side, her hand in mine. Margie took my other hand as we walked.

"Bea shared your secrets with me. You better be good to her. We Japanese know how to use knives. She'll cut you three ways if you do her wrong."

"Three ways?"

"Three ways...wide, deep, and often," Margie enunciated each word with a smile.

I got the picture.

Margie's tall, freckled boyfriend, Alex McLaren, joined us and we spent the day playing single-deck pinochle. Later, Alex and I visited while the girls fixed dinner.

"You're a lucky man," Alex said. We clanked our beer bottles together in a salute to my good fortune.

"Then you know?"

"Yes, Margie told me. She and I are getting married next year when I finish school at University of Pacific."

* * *

On the way home from Stockton, Bea asked, "Do you really, really love me, Pat?"

"Oh, Babe, I love you more than a fat kid loves ice cream!"

Turning halfway around in her seat, she punched me on the shoulder before speaking.

"Make love to me then, while we still can."

I pulled off the two-lane road in Livermore, into the leafless vines of the Concannon Vineyard. The end of the vineyard row was dark and the car became lost in the shadows. I fumbled for the condoms I'd purchased in San Francisco, where I was just another customer. At any of the drug stores in San Bruno, the nature of my purchase would unavoidable have spread and made problems for us both.

"You don't need those. Margie helped me get something from a doctor."

"Where is it?"

"I'm wearing it," was her quick reply before we joined.

I retrieved a plaid wool blanket from the trunk of my dad's 1937 Buick and spread it across the wide back seat. We made love, comfortable in the back seat of the car, then lingered in our warm embrace. My head was on an arm rest, Bea's head on my shoulder as I drank in the smell of her hair.

"Margie told me to keep my air of mystery I should never let you see me completely naked. I think I'll wear a hat, maybe. Would that keep me mysterious?"

"Always," I replied and squeezed her hands.

* * *

With only four days left until I departed for Keyport, my time was filled with last visits to school friends and neighbors. The railroad had given me this last week off—my career on hold until the government no longer had need of me. We made love only once more before I left—in her room on a sunny Thursday afternoon, as she played hooky from work. I remember her panic when the front door of the house opened and closed unexpectedly.

"Hide, hide, hide!"

I was standing naked in her closet, my clothes at my feet, as her mother came to the bedroom door. Bea opened the door wearing only her full-length plaid wool coat buttoned to her throat. Mother and daughter spoke as my heart pounded.

"You're blind like your father! Why do you think I had matched you with Russell? Did you think that was just your own good luck? I did it for you, you foolish girl. I did it all. You could have been the respected wife of a successful merchant, and been safe with your own people."

Mrs. Sakai was upset, spitting out her words.

"Mother, you didn't!"

I heard outrage in Bea's voice, followed by the sound of a slap. I felt sweat running down my sides. My hand went to the door knob and I pushed the closet door partway open. As I looked over Mrs. Sakai's back, I saw Bea's hand was covering her red cheek. Bea's eyes caught mine and she gave a tiny shake of her head, bidding me to stay in the closet. I stepped back and silently closed the door.

"Just so you know, He sees you as exotic, a Geisha girl. Someday—when your novelty is gone—he'll leave you for one of his own kind. Wherever you live, you will never be an American. You'll always be Japanese in their eyes. Now all of my work, matching you with Russell, is all for nothing, you ungrateful, stupid child." Her mother's voice, both scornful and dismissive, cut me like a knife.

"It's already too late, Mother. I love him and he loves me. I will wait for him until we can be one. I'm not going to be the good Japanese wife you want me to be."

"I cannot help you anymore," her mother said, her voice sharp. Then I heard footsteps, followed by the loud slam of a door. Bea released me from the closet, her cheek now glowing red from the blow.

"You better go now."

Dressing hurriedly, I waited near the closet door until Bea— peeking out into the hall—saw that her mom was in another part of the house.

Putting her finger to her lips, she pointed to the window. Neither of us said anything about the exchange I had overheard.

* * *

The next morning at the San Bruno train station our goodbyes were short. I stood with a pigskin suitcase, borrowed from my dad, in one hand and my arm wrapped around Bea with the other. She leaned in and spoke softly.

"What my mother said—about Russell—I never knew. I thought it just happened. I'm so sorry."

I said nothing but connected what her mother had said yesterday to my memory of a conversation I'd overheard years before.

"It's okay. You and I were both just kids. She was the adult. I guess she thought she was doing the best thing for you. I'm just so glad you decided that she was wrong."

"I love you, Pat. Thank you for saving me."

"I love you, too. That's how I can face leaving you now. We'll be together soon… I promise."

I turned and kissed her. Then, taking three steps over to my parents, I kissed Mom, hugged Dad and boarded the train.

"Do a good job, son, and write your mom. She worries."

10.   Seattle, 1940

The train trip from San Bruno to Seattle took a little more than 32 hours. Arriving late Saturday afternoon, I was eager to leave the recliner seat, long infused with cigar smoke, which had been both my seat and bed. When I got off the train my Uncle Burt was waiting for me on the wooden platform.

"It's good to see you, son. Your dad let me know when you'd be arriving," and he stepped forward to offer his hand, man to man.

"I'll take you to the Keyport ferry on Monday morning. You'll probably want to be there early on your first day to find your way around so you know where you need to be."

"That's swell, Unc. Have you ever been to Keyport? Do you have any idea where I go once I get off the ferry?"

"I've been to Keyport. The ferry lands right next to the town's one store. That puts you less than a hundred yards from the front gate. Do you know who to check in with when you get to Keyport?"

I pulled out the letter and read aloud.

"*Present this letter along with proper identification to the guard at the Main Gate. You will be escorted to Building No. 1 for your orientation, fingerprinting, and work assignment. Please arrive on time.*"

"What's the pay?"

"I get a hundred a week plus a monthly housing allowance of fifty."

"Good money," he commented.

* * *

Standing at the gate Monday morning—February 15, 1940—were 18 new hires like myself. Looking over the group, I

59

picked out a nearby friendly face. Offering his hand, he introduced himself.

"Andy Muldrow. I'm glad to meet you."

"Pat McBride," I said, shaking his hand.

I chose to listen more than talk, and I was happy to hear Andy's story while we passed the time waiting to enter the torpedo station. He was from Hot Springs, Arkansas.

"Say, where's home for you anyway?"

"A little town you probably never heard of, but basically I'm from San Francisco," I said.

"I was a machinist in Fort Smith, Arkansas. I hoped to get placed in the munitions works at McAlester, Oklahoma, but here I am. Such is life," Andy shrugged, his smile never dimming.

Andy had arrived four days before I did. He had found a room to rent in the home of two brothers, Jack and George Kuhns—bachelor farmers. Andy rode the bus in from nearby Poulsbo. The government had established a bus route that came and went between the torpedo station and Poulsbo, Silverdale and Bremerton—all to support Keyport's expanding workforce.

"Down home, I never would have thought the Navy would have me bunked up with two Kuhns. That is just not our way back home in Hot Springs." Andy was smiling at his own play on words.

I gave him a hard stare. "Really?" I asked.

Not getting a laugh or smile from me, he continued with a more self-deprecating question.

"Where do you think I can get possum around here? Back in Arkansas, we love to eat possum."

Then he just grinned at me. Andy had sent me a message. Despite the stereotype of Arkansas residents offered in the comic strip, "Li'l Abner." He was smart, clever and had a wicked sense of humor.

"Andy, blow it out your ass." I smiled, appreciating the jokes even if the racial humor made me uncomfortable. But Andy, like my dad, meant no particular offense to anyone— including Negroes. He just thought it was funny.

We milled around outside the open gate, attentive to the directions of the two gate guards. Finally, things got started, and we followed the NCO who guided us to the personnel office of the torpedo station. At the door our guide spoke up.

"Fellas, go on in and take a seat. Have your employment letters ready and the clerk will be with you directly. Welcome to Keyport. We're glad to have you here."

One by one we were called from the waiting area to the counter. When it was my turn, I presented my papers and the clerk pulled my file folder.

"You're assigned to Building 73. Go through the door on your right for fingerprinting and a set of pictures—one for the file and one for your ID badge."

After prints and photos were taken, I was sent back to the waiting area. When the last of our group had been processed, we were ushered into an adjoining room. There we sat facing a small stage. Soon the station commander entered, and I sat more erect in my seat.

"Men, welcome to the Naval Torpedo Station at Keyport. I am Station Commander Charles Munson. Welcome aboard. Tomorrow you will receive your identification badges. The badge shows your assigned building number and your picture. For security reasons, you are only permitted to be in your assigned work place and other approved common areas. This morning you will go to the payroll office to get set up there. Any of you who need assistance finding quarters will find a housing assistance office located next to payroll. After that you will go for a tour of the station, so you will know not only the location of your individual work area, but also the canteen, smoking areas, store, clinic and bomb shelters. Your work is vital to our country. You'll be well paid, you'll work hard, and you will help us stay strong. Again, welcome aboard!"

After the commander left the stage there was a brief silence. The 18 of us glanced around, some of us talking to other newcomers. Turning to my right, I greeted the stocky, olive-skinned guy in the next seat. He smiled and introduced himself.

"Call me Duano," he said. "My full name is a tongue twister and after three drinks I can't even say it myself, let alone spell it."

"Pat McBride from San Francisco, and this guy next to me is Andy Muldrow," I said, offering my hand. Andy leaned across me and also shook hands with Duano.

"I'm from Trenton, New Jersey. How about you?" he asked Andy.

"Arkansas," Andy replied.

The relaxed moment ended abruptly when a voice from the back of the theater grabbed our attention.

"Okay men, if you'll follow me, we'll get started. I'm Captain Olson, chief of security here at the station."

We followed him to the payroll office and then on to the housing office to be processed. The housing assistance office manager—an apple-cheeked matron overly fond of her lilac perfume—greeted us warmly. "Boys, you take a seat and start filling out these forms so I'll know how much space you'll need."

When my turn arrived, I told her I was single and wanted to be as close to work as possible.

"Can you pay $40 a month? How do you feel about sharing, if we get you a place here in Keyport, hon? It's a newly remodeled two-bedroom, so you'd have your own room, but share the rest of the place with another fella. Do you know anybody in your group who might want to share this space?"

After a quick "Yes, ma'am," I was given a referral card:

See Mrs. Lena Olson, Keyport Mercantile, shared housing; $40 per month each.

"Duano, the lady has a two-bedroom place in Keyport. You interested?"

"Sure," he replied as he joined me with the housing lady.

* * *

With our pay details all arranged and housing taken care of, the group followed Capt. Olson on our initial tour.

"Tomorrow you'll report to your assigned building after picking up your ID badge back at the reception center where we started. Each building is run by a naval officer. Over him is a civilian Bureau of Ordnance foreman. The naval officer is about as useful as tits on a boar hog, but he's there. You answer to your civilian foreman, but try not to piss off the Navy."

The station grounds were laid out on a small peninsula stuck out into Liberty Bay. Each building had a large version of its identifying number painted on its upper corner facing the street. Running from building to building was a network of narrow-gauge rail tracks. The tracks ran inside and right through many of the buildings. The captain explained a fully assembled torpedo weighed almost 3,300 pounds; the rails were our means of moving torpedoes from point to point.

"Muldrow and McBride, you'll work here, Building 73," he said, consulting his clipboard.

Our tour group just happened to find the two supervisors for Building 73 smoking outside the door. Bill Glasscock represented the Bureau of Ordnance, and Lt. J.G. Raymond Majeski was the naval officer assigned to our building.

Capt. Olson concluded the tour back at the main gate and we were set free for the day.

* * *

"Hey, shall we go look at the place in town?" I asked Duano.

"Sure," he replied.

Duano and I walked the one block from the main gate to the store. Keyport Mercantile was the largest building in town, sitting up and off to the right of the wooden ferry pier. Out front was the town's only gas pump, with Richfield's 'Flying A' brand. Inside display cases, each with a glass top, lined the walls of the large room. Groceries filled the center aisles. A free-standing stack of quart beer bottles nestled in wooden boxes stood at the end of one grocery counter. The shelves covering the walls of the store were neatly stacked with various categories of goods, toiletries and patent medicines. On top of a display sat the "*Tacoma Tribune*" newspaper and a basket of fresh eggs.

A pleasant, middle-aged woman greeted us. "Hello, boys, how can I help you?"

I held out the housing referral card.

"I'm Mrs. Olson, your landlady. My home is upstairs, here, above our store, and the rental is out back." As we followed her out behind the store, the sharp notes of chicken manure, familiar to me from my grandparents' farm, announced themselves.

Just two blocks from the bay, the low-tide smells had given way to the barnyard odors. What we saw—charitably speaking—was a remodeled chicken coop with a small covered porch facing off toward the station. A fenced chicken yard and coop backed up to the store, making up a large portion of the rental's view. Visible behind our new digs was the familiar profile of an outhouse.

Crossing the small front porch, we found a simple interior consisting of two bedrooms and a living room-kitchen combination with a sink, counters covered in sheet tin, cupboards of white painted wood, a four-burner propane stove and a small refrigerator. A table with two chairs completed the utilitarian décor of the room.

I looked over at Duano and asked what he thought of the place. He replied with an affirmative nod of his head.

"This will be fine, Mrs. Olson."

"When do you want to move in?"

"Move in tomorrow, Duano?"

Duano nodded his agreement and the matter was settled. Mrs. Olson extracted two house keys from the pocket of her sweater and handed them to us.

Housing now arranged, we decided to explore the rest of our new town. We took some time to have a look at our new surroundings. A loose three-block matrix of small houses and farms filled out the wooded, rolling hills that lined the seven miles of road back to the larger community of Poulsbo. Such was metropolitan Keyport, a small, functional stop before entering the torpedo station.

First, we went into Smith's Café, the local diner, to find a familiar setting with round stools along the counter and six small tables. The familiar smells of apple and cinnamon wafted from a freshly baked pie, replaced the outdoor smell of low tide.

Behind the cash register were pictures of the café's owner and only waitress at about the age of 6. She was dressed in a cowgirl outfit and standing next to a pony in front of the low stone walls by the main gate of the torpedo station.

We each ordered pie and coffee from the waitress, who appeared to have aged about 40 years since being photographed in her cowgirl outfit.

Duano introduced himself. "We're new hires."

"Welcome to Keyport. I'm Florence."

"I'm Pat. We're renting the little house behind the mercantile from Mrs. Olson."

Crossing to the opposite end of the diner, I inspected the Post Office. The counter tucked in the corner of the café was topped by a small arch of decorative bars reminiscent of a bank teller's cage. At the window, I said "Hello," to the man inside.

"Hello, I'm Dan, the postmaster, for all that means. I'm only here four hours a day, 10 until 2, five days a week. If you miss me and need stamps or whatever, just ask Florence."

11.   Keyport, December, 1940

I had now been at Keyport for almost 11 months. I asked Bea if she could get away to come and visit me now that I was finally settled in and had the money to cover her expenses. I thought she could stay in Seattle and I could ride the ferry over and back each day during her visit. As Christmas neared, I waited for her answer. I got Bea's letter shortly after New Year's Day.

December 22, 1940
Dear Pat,
I miss you terribly and hope you feel the same, as that will make my news even better. Cousin Margie, who is now Mrs. Alex McLaren, is going to help. She has invited me along on a March trip to see her aunt and uncle in Seattle. The trip will be in the early spring, but that is all I know for now except we'll be taking the train. Auntie and Uncle are older and live in a one bedroom apartment in Seattle. Margie and I will arrange a hotel room to share. I get to play tourist, or maybe just play, while Margie visits her relatives. I'm so excited to think of visiting you.
Love, Bea

Bea and Margie timed their travel to arrive in Seattle on the Sunday noon train. I met them at the rail station and piled their bags into a taxi. We rode the eight short blocks to the Eimoto Hotel on the edge of Nihonjim Machi, the "Japan Town" area of the city. After checking in and getting their bags up to the room, Margie announced she and Bea were expected for dinner at the home of her Aunt Shigeko and Uncle Kikunatsu.

"Bea, you don't look well at all, you know. I'm going to make an apology for you," Margie said, while she collected her purse, coat and hat.

"I think you should go straight to bed. I'll be back after 9 p.m., but not a minute before."

We smiled as she left, and I was finally alone with Bea for the first time in fourteen months.

"I'm so glad you're here," was all I could think to say.

We sat down on one of the room's twin beds. I hugged her and began kissing her neck, face and ears. Burying my face in her hair, I drank in her scent and the warmth of her touch. She returned my kisses as we lay down on the bed, still holding each other in a tight hug.

"What I missed most about our being apart was the absence of touch and the way your touching me makes me feel. I'm so glad you're here. I love you so very much."

"We love each other very much," she corrected and whispered, "Just hold me."

With her head on my shoulder, our bodies aligned on the bedspread. Bea spoke.

"I need to visit the bathroom. Will you please turn down the bedspread and pull the curtains?"

Rising from the bed, I folded back the spread and turned down the blanket and sheet. At the window, I closed the sheer curtains, filtering the afternoon light and blocking any view into the room. The bathroom door opened and in the half-light Bea walked across the room and lay down beside me, where we made love, hard and fast, then lay pressed together.

"You're not done, you know. Love me again," she said.

I did.

Afterward we bathed and dressed. I made an effort to remake the bed and opened the curtains. We went outside into the early evening and chose a small restaurant in the middle of a city block. We ate a spaghetti dinner, drank red wine, and shared, through our pervasive garlic breath, all the feelings that words on paper could not convey.

"This is a beautiful place. I love the hills and the bay. They're so much like San Francisco. I could live here," she said, as she looked out over the harbor.

"Soon, I hope," I said, taking her hand from across the table.

We passed the next three days in similar fashion, sharing every possible moment. I went to Seattle after my shift and caught the last ferry back to Keyport each night. During the day, Bea visited Margie's relatives, shopped in Nihonjin Machi, and saw the sights of Seattle and Puget Sound.

On Wednesday night, our last together, the three of us went out to dinner. I held Bea's hand as we walked down toward the harbor. The March night was brisk and the pedestrians were all in long, warm coats and hats. Tweed coats and fedoras seemed to be the uniform of the day for men. The women showed style beyond mere function in their coats: fur if the couple was prosperous or heavy broadcloth, if family finance emphasized performance over fashion.

I saw strangers looking at us, holding their view for an extra second, but quickly averting their gaze if they saw one of us looking back. While nothing was said, we felt the subtle message of disapproval.

"Jerks," I said, annoyance creeping into my tone.

Bea didn't speak, but squeezed my hand tighter.

"Margie, I appreciate your setting up this visit and keeping our secret. I know the law technically makes it illegal in California to marry someone of a different race. Did you and Alex have any trouble with the authorities?"

"No one even batted an eye about us marrying."

"I'm relieved to hear that. I figured I would just tell anyone who has a problem with our marrying that Bea is an Eskimo. She does look a bit like an Eskimo, don't you think? Here, watch her kiss me by rubbing my nose."

We all laughed. Bea moved ahead on the sidewalk, turned and stretched up to my height, then rubbed her nose to mine.

"See, 100 percent Eskimo. I'll grant the nose kissing is a little strange, but have you ever seen her eat whale blubber? Now *that* is really strange."

This final comment earned me a slap on the shoulder from Bea, who rolled her eyes and looked away from me

"Pay no attention to the crazy stranger," she said to Margie.

"Seriously, are we okay? I worry you're going to find someone...someone there...with me away for so long," I said.

"Nope, you're stuck with me...unless you find some blonde or some other Eskimo girl to keep you warm up here."

"Never, babe."

"My mother doesn't talk to me very much, except to tell me you'll find somebody else, some blonde white girl with big breasts. I don't think she will ever accept my being with a non-Japanese. But, I'm fine. I just miss you."

"I miss you, too." I hugged Bea for a long moment, resting my chin on top of her black hair.

At the end of the evening, we walked together back to their hotel. Margie said goodbye in the lobby and went up to their room. Unspoken between us was their departure at 9 a.m. tomorrow.

"I told you I'd be waiting for you. Our plans are coming together—my job, our savings, and the fact you like the Seattle area. I've been thinking that we could get married at Christmas. By then, I'll be able to get a couple days off."

"Yes, I want us to be together," she said.

"Think about it, and tell me in your letters what you would like. I'll do whatever I must to make it happen. It's really hard to say goodbye, so I'm just going to go."

We shared one final kiss, then she walked into the elevator. I turned and headed down the hill towards the ferry.

* * *

Bea wrote that during her train trip home, she told Margie about our plan to marry sooner rather than later. They concluded we should be married New Year's Day, 1942. Who was I to argue?

I told her I had to be the one to ask her father. I reached Mr. Sakai by phone that night and received his permission to marry Bea. We talked about the prohibition against interracial marriage and how the law had not stopped Alex McLaren and Margie Watanabe.

"Sir, if we have to, we can say Bea is an Eskimo. We'll find a way until the stupid law changes."

"Patrick," Mr. Sakai said, "I think you will be an asset to our family. Even my very traditional brother, Saburo, who is back in Japan, will come to see your marriage to Beatrice is a good thing. Saburo may visit Hawaii later this year. Who knows? If things go well for him, maybe he'll be able to make it all the way to the West Coast."

As the months rolled by, Bea's letters kept me updated on the details of our wedding. Other than requesting leave for one week starting December 29, I left all the planning to my intended. I dutifully replied, "Sounds great," to each item Bea put forth, happy to be far enough away that I could absent myself from the details of the planning.

May 25, 1941:

Your Mom and I looked at wedding dresses in San Mateo. I think this is almost more work for her than it is fun for me. I'll be a vision in white satin. Don't you dare say a word about the white dress!

July 19, 1941:

Dad keeps checking with me about the flowers he is getting for the wedding. We decided on red and white roses because I love their fragrance and Dad says the colors remind him of his childhood in Japan. He worries, since our own fields will not have any blooms yet. He is reaching out with his long arm into a mafia of Japanese flower growers he knows along the border in Arizona. His friends have all promised their blooms will be here, even if they have to deliver them by airmail early Sunday morning!

12.   Keyport, November, 1941

Sitting on our porch one late fall day, I told Duano about Bea and our plans to marry. He made no comment about her being Japanese, except to smile broadly. Pointing my way with two fingers held out like pistols.

"You've got yellow fever, my friend. I had it once, too, but just the twenty-four hour kind."

"You're right. I've got a terminal case."

"I get it. I didn't mean anything by the yellow fever crack— it's just an expression. I'm sure she's a great gal."

In my weekly letters home, I had told my folks about Keyport, Duano and Andy. The money I enclosed continued to be deposited in my account at our bank. The converted chicken coop, which I now called home, had become safe and familiar as the routines of daily life had fallen into place. With Mrs. Olson's approval, we had been keeping our own small flock of chickens since spring. After dinner I filled my time with Duano, usually with pinochle and conversation at our kitchen table. Our connection seemed to deepen when we discovered both of our dads had been bootleggers.

"What did your dad want you to be when you grew up?" I asked.

"He wanted me to go to law school. He thought this was where the real money in crime was and also a nice fit with his business. But I wanted to be a garbage man. It's steady work. We've got family connections to the business and it's useful to have a place to dump things." He delivered that line with a steady tone and no hint of irony.

"And your mom, did she want her little boy to grow up to be the garbage man?"

"I don't think her hopes for me were ever that specific or lofty. I think she just hoped I'd become a priest, or at least a silk purse."

"I was just remembering how Bea taught me to dance so I could take her to the bank's Christmas party."

"So tell me," Duano gestured with his hands for me to continue.

"I was informed we weren't going if I couldn't dance. Bea had stayed in school and graduated in June 1938. She had little trouble getting her first job—training to be a teller at the local Bank of America.

"She told me, 'There's a Christmas party at the bank on the Friday before Christmas. If you're going to be my date, then you must know how to dance.'

"Duano, I didn't know how to dance. The only school dance we ever went to, all we did was hug in the dark and rock back and forth from side to side. It was kind of embarrassing.

"So she says, 'Don't worry, I'll teach you. You'll only have to learn one slow dance, a waltz or foxtrot, and one other. But something faster, maybe like the Balboa swing they do in San Francisco. Come on, it'll be fun. We'll practice at my house.'

"I was so nervous. Bea brought a small record player from her room, and we practiced to a few tunes where I could hear the beat—played over and over—until I was a passable dance partner. She really encouraged me, saying, 'You're doing much better, just try not to count the beat out loud.' She was so sweet about it." I chuckled to myself at the memory.

"I bought a blue suit and somehow managed to get a corsage pinned on the shoulder of her pink satin gown without stabbing her. She clutched my arm and showed me off to all her co-workers, seeming as proud of me as I was proud to be with her. When we danced—she gracefully and me clumsily— to the romantic strains of "Blue Moon," she kissed my cheek and whispered in my ear, saying, 'You're doing wonderfully. You're so handsome. I love you, Pat.'"

Duano listened, sitting in silence, his head bent and eyes downcast.

* * *

With each passing month, the conflict in Europe and Japanese aggression in the Far East grew. All the while the Keyport's workforce continued to expand. Bea's folks were upset about what they saw as the increasing number of anti-Japanese editorials in the San Francisco papers. Every day there seemed to be some new hostile action, either by our government or by the Japanese. Bea pretended not to be concerned, but as she reported the worries of her parents, I couldn't help but believe the same fears to be her own. As the months rolled on, the small insults and the separation of America into "us" and "them" grew worse. Then came Pearl Harbor, and it all turned to shit.

"The milk man won't deliver to us anymore." Then, "The locals won't cash Dad's checks anymore." Bea's letters became harder to read and my reassurances probably sounded more hollow, if they were believed at all.

13.   Keyport, Early June, 1942

It was now six months into the war. All the Japanese on the West Coast were subject to the 10 p.m. curfew Gen. DeWitt had imposed. The regular letters from my mom and from Bea did nothing to ease my fears about how the country had turned on some of its own citizens.

June 10, 1942

Dear Pat,

Just time for a short note today, my love. Dad and I went to a war bond rally last night. We bought another $20 bond. Everybody who bought a bond got a little red leather case to hold their war ration stamp books. We're not supposed to trade stamps with anyone but some of us do anyway, for things that we really want or need. The Herald published a notice asking everyone to bring any rubber we had, like old tires, to the fire station for the war effort. I took in the little tire-shaped ash tray that I got from the Seaside Oil service station. Every little bit helps, I guess. We can't get any tires for the Buick at the moment. The paper says that the government is hard at work on synthetic rubber, now that the supply from Indochina is cut off. Dad and I are fine and proud of you. Mr. Sakai says to pass along his hello.

Love, Mom

Andy, Duano and I were having a beer after work. As we sat on the porch of the mercantile on this warm June evening, I thought a break might help clear my head. Then I saw the flyer.

!!Attention—Soldiers, Sailors, Marines and Defense Workers!!
Republic Pictures wants to honor you with a sneak preview of
our newest movie.
All persons in uniform or with proper ID admitted free.
Thank you from Republic Pictures.

Beneath the banner headline was a list of locations and dates. Tonight's showing was in Poulsbo.

"Guys, I need to get away from Keyport for a night. Maybe you could use a break, too. How about we go to the free show in town?"

"What do you think will be playing?" Duano asked me, while he wiped foam from his upper lip.

"Who cares? Andy, what do you think?"

"Well, if there'll be beer at the end of the movie, I'm in," said Andy.

"It's settled, then."

We took the bus into Poulsbo for the show. The marque read:

Tonight, Sneak Preview—Service Appreciation Night.

A *"News Parade"* newsreel started the show, with the announcer reading a voice-over narrative of scenes provided by the government.

"Yanks bomb Tokyo! April 18, 1942, the aircraft carrier Hornet steams toward Japan hoping to get within four hundred miles of the enemy undetected. Parked on the after-deck of the Hornet are 16 Mitchell B-25 bombers commanded by Colonel Jimmy Doolittle. Never before have these huge planes been launched from a carrier. Closer to enemy waters, a Jap patrol boat sights the fleet and is quickly sunk. Rushing to take off before any warning from the patrol boat flashed the news of our fleet in the vicinity

*of the home islands, all 16 planes got off into the wind as
the carrier's deck pitched upward. The 16 raiders split off
to separate destinations, attacking their military targets
in Tokyo, Nagoya and Yokahama. Every plane hit its target
with a 2,000-pound bomb load. Low on gas, 15 of the 16
raiders landed safely in China or Russia. After four months
of the Jap having his way in the Pacific, the Navy gives them
the first taste of what is to come and keep coming until
they are obliterated!"*

Both men and women erupted from their seats. A shower of
popcorn fluttered down, launched into the air by the crowd's
triumphant gestures. The crowd cheered the newsreel showing
Japanese cities crowned with smoke and wreathed in flame.
Clapping and cheering, the collection of strangers became one.
The three of us stood and joined in the celebration. We were all
caught up in the moment. It was so good to feel powerful, even
for a brief instant.

The sneak preview movie was *"Flying Tigers."* John Wayne
starred as the leader and organizer of the Flying Tigers, officially
the American Volunteer Force. As Capt. Jim Gordon, he resigns
his commission in our Army and goes to China in 1937 to help
build the Chinese air force. He falls in love and marries a
beautiful Chinese woman. His unit—the Flying Tigers—are all
American volunteer pilots and morally everything the Japanese
were not. The Jap pilots machine-gun civilians. The Flying Tigers
parachute supplies to makeshift hospitals. The Japanese strafe
to death an American pilot as he hangs helpless in his parachute.
The Japanese pilot curled his lip and taunt our heroes.

"You're surprised that I speak your language," snickers the
Japanese pilot. "I learned it at Stanford University. Hah! Hah!
Hah!"

Bang!-bang!-bang!

"Die, Yankee bandit!" he sneers, while machine-gunning a wounded opponent's parachute.

The movie managed to give us what we expected and wanted—Japs that were treacherous, vicious and without any honor or humanity. We all cheered when the Japanese pilot died in a flaming crash. At that moment, I hated Imperial Japan as much as anyone in the theater.

* * *

Before the attack on Pearl Harbor, the gates and grounds at Keyport had been guarded by two-man patrol units from the Bureau of Ordnance. Now these guards were outside the fence and the Main Gate. Inside the station, Marines patrolled. They carried submachine guns and their numbers were augmented with patrol dogs. Civilian contractors were working at multiple places around the station, setting forms for concrete defensive positions. Some of the emplacements would hold anti-aircraft guns. Other partially-buried roofed structures would be for machine guns or artillery pieces to point out toward the water, or west toward the hills.

We were all afraid. The fears that Bea and my mom both shared in their letters matched my worries about our future. Distant bad news from the war fronts seemed only to be mirrored and amplified by more local events. I almost gave up reading the *"Tacoma Tribune;"* a simple peek at the front page was enough.

June 20, 1942.

Lighthouse Shelled by Jap Sub

Canadian authorities confirmed that the Estevan Point Lighthouse on Vancouver Island was attacked in the early morning hours yesterday. Damage to the facility was not disclosed, but authorities did confirm that between 25 and 30 shells were fired by a submarine. The attacker had slipped away by the time naval forces arrived from Victoria, BC.

June 21, 1942.

Fort Stevens Shelled!

Portland authorities confirmed that the Fort Stevens defense complex at the mouth of the Columbia River came under attack from a marauding Jap submarine in the early hours of June 20. The only reported damage from the 17 shells that struck was to the baseball field on the complex grounds.

"Hey, Pat, here's something about your hometown and a Japanese spy. You need to see this."

The story was on the second page of the "Tacoma Tribune", but without Duano I might have missed it.

June 20, San Bruno, California

Oishi Sakai, a local flower grower, was killed at the family garden shop in downtown San Bruno. Mr. Sakai was shot and killed by federal agents who came to take him into custody for questioning as a suspected agent of the Japanese government. Sakai was armed with a knife, which he drew when agents arrived.

Sakai's wife and children, who witnessed the shooting, were not hurt in the deadly encounter and were taken into custody pending relocation from the West Coast.

The charges against Mr. Sakai, if proven, would have been the first arrest of an enemy agent on American soil. Prior to the confrontation, the FBI had searched a storage shed in Linda Mar belonging to Sakai. Tipped off by a suspicious neighbor, agents found lanterns believed to have been used to communicate with lurking Japanese submarines. Also discovered in the search was a quantity of poison. According to confidential sources, Sakai was believed to be planning to poison the city of San Francisco water supply. The city water department property, Crystal Springs Reservoir, was accessible from the Sakai property via a dirt road.

Mr. Fred Craig, a fellow flower grower, advised this reporter, "Sakai would take lanterns down the valley. This looked suspicious, so I followed him once and saw him take the lanterns to the isolated Hidden Cove Beach next to Pedro Point. I have been trying for years to add his field to mine, but now I see he needed the isolated location to communicate with the submarines, hide his poison cache, and be close to the lakes.

"I happened to be walking along the creek that is the south border of his place and mine. I found a burn pile with scraps of pictures of Japs in uniform. I brought 'em to the feds when I told 'em about Sakai. I'm glad I was able to help catch him in time."

I read the article again with disbelief. If I had read that my dad had been arrested for bookmaking, illegal gambling or liquor violations, I would not have been surprised. But the "*Tribune*" story was impossible, given my years of knowing Mr. Sakai. The only believable part of the news story was that Craig's scheming covetous behavior had gotten a man that I respected killed. I had to believe that all Mr. Sakai was guilty of was being Japanese on the West Coast.

Mom's letter of July 3 reached me July 10.

Dear Pat,

I know you have been trying to contact Bea. I'm afraid the awful news that surprised us all may be true after all. We

81

just don't know. Enclosed is the story as it appeared in the "San Bruno Herald." I don't know if it is any different from what you've seen. I visited Bea and her mother at Tanforan on Monday. She asked for fabric to make a room divider and curtains. I'm going to bring her the fabric tomorrow and some Hexol to help get the horse smells out. They are in one of the stables that we could see across the track from the grandstand. With Mr. Sakai's death and the family gone, I'm afraid that in the minds of most local folks, he is certainly a spy in death, even if he wasn't in life.

I've clipped the pictures that were in the paper showing the search of Mr. Sakai's shed. Also, I've enclosed another story about the Sakai's store burning down. The police and fire departments are not investigating the fire as arson. The store had been closed since the Sakais were taken. I went by the store after the fire. All of the beautiful flowers out back in the lath houses were dead on the ground amid the ashes. In the ashes inside the store, I found the pretty ceramic vase that I admired so often and brought it home for safe keeping.

Dad and I are well. We're getting along fine with the rationing. Dad misses coffee but it is nothing we can't live without. Like most folks, we planted a small garden in the back yard since what we grow is extra for us and not rationed. Your money at Bank of America is safe, and with the last deposit the balance is now $3,225. Remember Betty, Bea's friend at the bank? She says hello. We love you and are proud of your work.

Love, Mom

The second story in the "San Bruno Herald" led with a banner headline—*Jap Owned Business Burned*—above a picture showing the scorched remains of the building. A second smaller image showed charred sticks that had once been camellias and rhododendrons standing in pots amid the ruins of the lath house.

I had to unfold the pictures of the Sakai flower field showing the aftermath of the supply shed search. Seven dark sedans and an armored car surrounded the shed. Lines of tire tracks marked the black earth of the field. The picture showed armed men— shotguns at the port-arms position—in a protective outer ring, as two figures, enclosed in white rubber suits with hoods, wearing gauntlet style gloves and gas masks, carried large glass bottles to the armored car. In small print below the image was the caption:

"Feds remove poisons from spy hideout just three miles from San Francisco water supply!"

I knew what was being loaded into the armored car. The big brown glass bottles were the insecticides that I had helped apply to the fields, and that Mrs. Sakai sold in the garden store.

"Those assholes!" I cursed aloud.

"Who? Who's the asshole?"

"The good people of my home town, that's who. They burned down the store that was owned by Bea's parents."

"Yup, they sound like major assholes to me," Duano nodded, not glancing up from the daily comics page. "I'm sorry."

After Pearl Harbor, the mere accusation of spying was all most people needed to brand any Japanese person guilty. Bea and her family had been taken into custody after her father was shot. Now they were being held at Tanforan. If a letter from me to Bea was intercepted by the FBI or the Navy, it would bring suspicion on me or my family for consorting with the enemy. Fear had seized us all. None of the Sakai family was my enemy or anyone else's. But perception had become reality. The country, especially the West Coast, was absolutely terrified by the so-called "yellow menace".

"Duano, my mom says that she and Dad will go to Elko, Nevada, if the Japanese invade the West Coast."

"It's hard to even imagine the terror folks feel when they hear the government officials talking about stopping them at the Sierras or at the Grand Canyon," said Duano, shaking his head.

14.   Keyport, July, 1943

Mom's letters arrived regularly with news of home, family and what little she could tell me about the Sakais. I forwarded letters for Bea through Mom, asking that she hand deliver them to Tanforan.

Bea's messages to me filtered back by the same route, until the messages stopped in late April. Mom's letters only said she was not allowed to visit Tanforan anymore.

July 15, 1943

Dear Son,

Enclosed is a letter we received from Bea along with her letter to us. She asked that we pass it on to you. She was afraid that writing to you directly might get you in trouble.

They were relocated to the Tule Lake Camp in May, because Mr. Sakai was a suspected spy. Dad and I found Tule Lake on a California map.

You might remember driving up through northern California and into eastern Oregon on our way to Mount Rainier when you were ten. The camp is just below Klamath Falls, and ten miles east of the little town of Dorris, where we stopped for gas.

I've heard the camp is reserved for families suspected of being disloyal, or who had refused internment. I'm also sending you her note to us, as it has information that we've not seen in the papers and I know you would want to see it.

I hope everything is all right with you both, as your dad and I think the world of Bea and her family. We don't believe the awful things that people are saying about Mr. Sakai.

Love, Mom

July 7, 1943

Dear Mother McBride,

My family and I are so sad and ashamed about what has happened. We hope that our friends and neighbors can believe we have done nothing to hurt our country. Still, Dad's death and the fire at the store show me clearly how things are, even if I wish it were not so. Growing up in San Bruno had been so wonderful that I cry now when I think about what people must be thinking.

We were not allowed newspapers, nor to write for weeks, after they took us from Tanforan to the new camp at Tule Lake in May. As you maybe can see by the red "censored" stamp, all our mail is checked. I hope that not too much has been blacked out by the time you get this. I have come to know that the papers say my Dad was shot for pulling a knife on a federal agent. Truly, this is not so and I want you to know what really happened.

Dad, as always, had his little belt knife that he used to trim plants and bulbs. When the men rushed in, their guns were already drawn. We all stepped back, except Dad who stepped in front of us. Seeing the knife on his belt, one large man demanded that Dad "put the weapon down." Dad drew the knife and was offering it, handle first, to the big man, when another agent came through the door and just shot him. The shooter seemed indifferent, saying, "I stopped another Jap sneak attack!"

Curley was in front of Mom and at the pistol shot he growled and showed his teeth. The man who shot Dad screamed at us to "Hold that goddamn dog or I'll shoot him, too." I grabbed Curley by his collar and pulled him away. As old as he was, he still didn't want to leave my Mom. I held his muzzle closed as I knelt beside him and finally got him to be quiet. They took Curley from me when they took us away, promising to take him to the Humane Society. When they put us in the back seat of a big car, I heard another shot from inside our house. Probably Curley.

I wonder if they felt the same about shooting a Japanese man as they felt about shooting a dog.

The paper says Dad used the lanterns we had for working at twilight for signaling submarines. Mr. Craig must have seen Dad take a lantern to Hidden Cove to gather mussels because the low tide was late in the day. The pesticides we used on the flower fields were the poisons the paper says they claim to have found. I hope you can believe that we would not do any of the things the papers are reporting.

They sent us by train from Tanforan to Klamath Falls, and then by bus to the camp. The camp makes an ugly scar on this pretty part of the California high desert.

When we got here, we were presented with a loyalty oath to sign. Ernie and I, being citizens, signed the oath. Others, including Mom, refused to agree to two mandatory items. The two questions asked, "Are you willing to serve in the Armed Forces of the United States on combat duty wherever ordered?" and "Will you swear unqualified allegiance to the United States and faithfully defend the United States from any and all attacks by foreign or domestic forces, and forswear any form of allegiance or obedience to the Japanese Emperor, or any other foreign government, power, or organization?"

Some folks who were born in Japan, like Mom, actually want to go back to Japan when the war is over. She believes that this country has turned its back on her. But she fears that the Issei, those born in Japan, might be deported now. Answering "yes" to either question would make them enemies to the Japanese if they were sent back, so she felt she was damned by whatever she did.

Tule Lake now has its own prison-within-a-prison for troublemakers like Mom. Congress directed the relocation authority to establish one "segregation camp", and they picked Tule Lake for the site. The segregation camp is separated from our relocation camp by a barbed wire barrier. She is confined in segregated isolation, they say because she refused to sign the oath and wants to go back to Japan after the war. I know that she is being treated more harshly because of what they think Dad did. I can visit her only once a week. It is the most awful part of this terrible place.

Ernie and I have one room here, and I am planting a late garden. He is part of a camp crew that is making the bare ground friendlier with gravel paths, a baseball diamond, and a playground for the children. I will write when I can and I pray for us all. Please send my note to Pat and I ask you please not to read it. I love you all.

Beatrice Sakai

I had to reread Mom's note to me and Bea's letter to my folks both twice to overcome my own disbelief of the events.

"Shit," I cursed. Finally, I read Bea's letter.

July 7, 1943

Dearest Patrick,

This is such a hard letter to write. Our karma has determined we are not to be together. I have never doubted your love for me, and you should never doubt my love for you. Everyone seems to have gone crazy and I see now that because we are different, we will never be able to be together. I see now that your country will never permit us to live the life we planned. Besides the killing of Dad and the imprisoning of Mom, the small acts of meanness by the staff hurt us so. Tule Lake and the other ten camps are all to protect you from us.

It will hurt us both too much to think we can have our beautiful life together, while everyone else is so afraid of my family name. I will forever hold the innocence you gave

me. Maybe in our next lives we will be together. I can't bear to see you or hear from you again. Goodbye my love.
Bea

Sitting on my bed in our little house and reading the letter from Bea over and over, I didn't cry or curse. After a while, my pain turned into emptiness and then the emptiness was replaced by anger. At that point my anger had yet to be focused on anyone or anything. I only knew that the rage filling me would be easier to stand than the grief.

"Our government is responsible for killing Mr. Sakai, interning the family and imprisoning Mrs. Sakai." The words I spoke became visible in my mind's eye, and seemed to hang there.

"They did it all," I sighed, managing to clear my mind.

These evils were not the work of lone individuals, but of a big faceless entity that I had never stopped to think about before. By accident, design or simply by being too willing to believe the accusations of a greedy neighbor who coveted Mr. Sakai's fields, our government had managed to utterly destroy the Sakai family and with it, my future.

I remembered that it was the Craig boys who had busted up the Posey Parade and the stink of the rotten fish they threw. I saw now the Craig boys were probably put up to their cries of "Japs go home." The Posey Parade attack could have been the opening shot in their father's campaign to get Mr. Sakai's field.

The cruelty of the neighbors who had burned the Sakai's store, the signs that read "No Dogs or Japs Allowed," and the other small acts of meanness Bea endured...made me ashamed. My secret fear was that Bea might be right about my country.

Bea had not stopped loving me, though. Her last letter said, "You should never doubt my love for you." She knew that I loved her, "But your country will never permit us to live the life we planned." I repeated her words aloud to myself over and over.

At that moment, I knew I could betray my country—and I would—if there was any chance of getting Bea back. I found it easy, perhaps too easy, to focus on my own hurt and the wrongs done to Mr. Sakai. He was my second father; the man who had taught me how to fish and defend myself. All I had to do was not look beyond what had been done to me and not examine what I was about to do. So plan I did. Examine what I was about to do? I did not. Without ever realizing, I had joined history's long line of zealots, driven by whatever was their particular righteous anger.

Duano was the only audience to my suffering as it grew deeper by the day. His hand on my shoulder, and the occasional "How ya doing?" or "One day at a time, brother," all showed his concern.

"I told my folks that our engagement was off, at least until after the war. She haunts me, Duano. I keep getting memories popping into my head. Like our first kiss, holding hands on the beach, or the first time we made love."

"Listen Pat, we need a night away from here. What do you say we go into Poulsbo for a drink in a real bar? I'll buy."

"Sounds like a plan, paisano."

Off we went to catch the bus that shuttled workers from their homes to the station. In Poulsbo we had three choices: Johnny and Red's, the Tip Top Club or the Cinnabar. Duano chose and we went into the Cinnabar. Beneath the chrome and red vinyl stools, sawdust covered the floor. The better for soaking up spilled beer or blood. Old men sat at tables playing dominoes. A lone stranger, perhaps a banker as suggested by the pressed brown slacks and the high polish on his brown shoes, stood alone at the bar. We strode up to the bar and drank one beer and then ordered another.

Their noise entered the bar, announcing their presence before they arrived. It was four sailors on liberty and out on the town. Based on the dolphin pins worn on their bright white shore uniforms, they were submariners.

"Make room, civilians, four warriors are about to tie up at your bar!"

The largest of the four men did the talking and seemed to be a leader with three willing followers.

"You heard the chief. Make way!" chimed in the smallest of the quartet. Each breath exhaled whiskey fumes that mingled with the smell of beer wafting from their skin and uniforms.

"Slide down the rail a bit, Duano. Let's give our brave fighting men some room," I said, smiling while we moved a few feet to the left along the bar.

We were nursing our second beer when the sailors placed their order.

"Beer and whiskey shots all around!"

Four beer mugs and four shot glasses arrived and were quickly emptied.

"Again, barkeep!" The second round appeared and was gone just as fast.

"Ready for another Pat? I'll buy."

"If you're buying, my Italian friend, I'd love to have another."

We held up our beer bottles, signaling that we were ready for more. We eased into our third beer while the sailors, already in their own third round of shots and beers, were getting louder and more animated.

"We're lucky to have made it back. I hope the yard takes their sweet time repairing our boat."

The speaker now was neither Mr. Big nor Mr. Small, but one of their two companions. The four voices continued becoming louder and harder to ignore.

"While we're in the neighborhood, we ought to find a way to get over to Keyport where those piece-of-shit Mark 14s are made." The other voices responded, signaling their agreement.

"Those civilians don't have any idea what it's like to have one of their fish go under a target or smack into the side of a Jap hull with a thud instead of a bang."

By their fourth round, Duano and I were tired of hearing about "the lazy, draft dodging sons-of-bitches that put that shit out, from their safety back in the rear."

"Duano, I think it's time to go. The neighborhood has gone to hell." I turned to leave and got bumped by a swinging forearm gesture from the sailor nearest me.

"Easy sailor," I said, taking a step back and leaning on the bar. "You and your pals can have the whole bar. We've got a bus to catch."

Mr. Small stepped out of the group and planted himself in front of me.

"You have a bus to catch? That wouldn't be the bus back to Keyport, would it, pal?"

I turned to the bar, putting my back to his rising tide of anger fueled by all the alcohol he had consumed. Duano stayed quietly at my side, ready to help if things got ugly, but trying not to fan the flames. I felt a poke in my back.

"Didn't your mommy teach you not to turn your back on someone that's speaking to you?"

The tall man with spit-shined brown shoes turned his head away and moved to the far end of the bar.

I felt another poke, harder this time. Still trying to avoid trouble, I ignored the jabs.

"Turn around asshole, I want you to look at me when I talk, you chicken-shit son-of-a-bitch."

When he grabbed my shoulder I turned, an empty long-neck beer bottle in hand. My backhand swing put the hard cylinder of glass against his neck, just below the jaw. Down he went; his eyes rolled back and lids descended before he collapsed onto the sawdust floor.

Mr. Big froze for a moment, then charged at me with outstretched arms. His hands flexed as he advanced, perhaps closing to fists or reaching out to grab me. He didn't make it. I stepped into his advance and grabbed his left wrist with both hands. It happened fast, his thumb rotated down until his wrist almost faced him. His elbow was now locked, and with one hand still on his wrist I pushed him to the floor at the elbow; his hand, wrist, and arm now locked into a single lever. He managed to turn his head so that the abrupt meeting of face and floor didn't break his nose or teeth. Blood started to trickle from one nostril, across his lip and down into the sawdust.

Duano fixed the two remaining sailors with a hard, unblinking stare and they froze. No one else in the place moved.

I held the sailor there and spoke into his ear. "You hear me okay down there?"

"Yes," I heard back, and the big man spit sawdust off his lips.

"Now, you probably can't see my work boots from your position so you might want to trust me on this. If I stomp your temple with the heel of my boot, you're dead. If I stomp your arm anywhere, it's broken. The elbow would be the worst for you, pain-wise." I leaned on the inverted wrist to make my point about pain.

"Do I still have your attention?" I said flexing the wrist one more time.

"Yes," he said, though it was delivered more as an audible gasp.

"Ok, here is what you'll do. I'll let you go this time, but if I ever get any more shit from you, your buddy or anyone else that knows you, you'll get the boot heel. Clear?"

"Yes."

"Say it again."

"Yes."

I released my hands and dropped his arm, raising a small cloud of dust.

"Out—now—and take your buddy. Drag him or carry him, it's up to you. When he comes around, let him know the deal you just made for all of you."

Stepping over the first attacker, I rejoined Duano at the bar.

"Where in the hell did you learn that shit? I'm from Jersey and I had my first fight at seven, but I've never seen the moves that you put on those two."

"I learned those and a few other things from Bea's dad. He helped me when I told him about how I was getting bullied in school."

"Amazing," was all Duano said.

"It's about time to catch our bus back to the station, paisano." As they left, I noticed the tall stranger smiling and nodding back in our direction.

Riding the bus back, I wasn't thinking about settling scores one asshole at a time. I would find my own way to even the score with the government. My hope, from re-reading Bea's last letter, was that she was rejecting what our country had become. She was not rejecting me. There was hope, if I could separate myself somehow, to make myself stand apart in her mind from our country. Then I might have some chance of getting her back and recapturing our dreams.

15.   Keyport, August, 1943

I sat at a lunch table overlooking the torpedo test-firing channel. A briny wind blew in across Liberty Bay. Suddenly the means of my revenge became clear to me. It was an epiphany, revealing itself in a moment. I knew I wasn't smarter than everybody else, which meant I'd have to be more careful than everyone else. Planning and patience would be my allies.

"Duano, are you still working as a torpedo fueler?"

"Yeah, but you know what? Those shit-heels send us perfectly good alcohol, then they ruin it by putting in poison. It's blue, for Christ sake! They call it denatured alcohol but, I ask you, what is up with that? If they only knew the damage to morale that this shit did to our brave fighting men overseas."

"They do that so you and your crew won't drink up the fuel."

I had seen the pallets of fifty-five gallon steel drums, painted all black with white skull-and-crossbones stenciled on each barrel above the identifying 'torpedo fuel' label. They arrived four to a pallet, drum head up. Each one had a threaded three-quarter-inch steel plug in the head and a larger threaded plug situated halfway up its cylindrical side. Once fueled, torpedoes rested in temporary storage until removed for test firing.

The two turbine blades inside were the beating heart of each torpedo. Their precise balance was critical to the power plant, and it was my job to perfect each blade. All of the other work on housings, shafts and gears would not amount to a pinch of shit if the all-important turbine blades were not perfect. The torpedoes were shipped from Keyport, already fueled. Only the arming of the warhead with a detonator was left to be accomplished before the submarines could use their weapons.

I knew that salt water caused electrolysis, making metal brittle and weak. The inspections of torpedoes after each test-firing included checking for even minor water leaks that could cause electrolysis. If I could put salt in the torpedo fuel, electrolysis would make the turbine blades brittle when they leapt from zero to twelve thousand RPMs in less than half a second. Our Mark 14 torpedoes used a fifty-fifty blend of alcohol and water that provided both the fuel and the steam needed to send our monster creations speeding forth to do their work. Inside the turbine, the extreme heat of the alcohol fire would vaporize any evidence of my act. Electrolysis was a slow, insidious worker, whose effects would show up later—not after a single test-firing. If the blades failed, the turbine failed and the torpedo would die harmlessly. I didn't need to sabotage every torpedo. After all, I didn't want the failures to be suspicious. Those few—or perhaps many—torpedoes that I stopped would go unnoticed among the forty percent failure rate that plagued the Mark 14s already. This was a way I could make the government pay. Was this rational thinking? Rational or irrational, at this point, I didn't care, for the twin emotions of love and hate both propelled me in the same direction.

My anger and dreams of revenge didn't dim my awareness. If I were caught in the act of sabotage, I could die in federal prison, tortured by vengeful inmates, or be shot where I stood by a Marine guard. I simply didn't care. Bea was worth the risk. Then it dawned on me that what I was considering would put more than my own life at risk. It would shame my parents, my uncles and Mr. Long. I imagined flames consuming my parent's house just as flames had devoured the Sakai's store. The bank would not hesitate to call in any loan on the family of a traitor during wartime. Either by flame or foreclosure, the community would find a way to cleanse itself of the McBride traitor. If I got caught, I knew the Sakai family would be further vilified 'Sakai, the spy, put the McBride kid up to the sabotage,' the neighbors would say. The thoughts of how my actions could affect others that I loved gave me pause. But, in the end, I spread an ointment of hate over my fears for others. I hoped that the salve might be enough to help my conscience scab over.

* * *

Everyone had to have an ID badge to get through the Main Gate and to enter their work station. My badge allowed me in to my duty station, Building 73, but no other. For the first several months after Pearl Harbor, the access rule was rigidly enforced by the Marine guards. By December 1942, the workers and the guards had settled into a predictable routine. The guards had been doing their various jobs for a year, and I had been working at Keyport for twenty-two months. The guards didn't become lax, but they did become more accommodating. I was known to them. I was part of the station's auxiliary defense force—someone willing to stand with them if the need arose. Most important, the Marines saw that I was known to the bosses.

By the first of May, 1943, I was once again able to enter Duano's building during the lunch break. I made it easy for the two Marines at the door to not see me as a threat. When I approached their door, my badge clearly visible, I set a standard of always asking permission before entering Duano's building.

"Fellas, may I go collect the Italian bum? It's lunch time."

Without being asked, I'd offer a view inside my open lunch box. A wave, a nod, or a wink, and I was inside Building 82, where the torpedoes were fueled. I would stop and make contact before entering the actual work area—sometimes visually, sometimes verbally—with one of the two building managers. I'd wait until recognized and then point to Duano. If I failed to see Duano, I'd mouth his name and shrug, signaling that I was asking for some clue about his whereabouts. Sometimes, once acknowledged by a building supervisor, I'd gesture that I'd wait in the locker-room. The fact that Duano was a frequent lunch-time visitor to my building as well established an element of normalcy to my movements between our two work stations.

* * *

Planning revenge meant discovering how to compromise torpedoes without compromising myself. I needed to know how much simple salt would be needed to produce electrolysis in the torpedo's inner workings. One of the reasons for the triple inspection of torpedoes was that the salinity of sea water was enough to cause problems. My first order of business was to know just how salty is seawater.

From my railroad days, I knew how sensitive boilers and turbines were to what is called hot corrosion. Our Mark 14 torpedoes were powered by miniature steam engines. The extreme heat of the boiler amplified the corrosive power of salts in the brackish waters of the West, which sometimes got into locomotive engines. The salt in the water melted at high temperatures and produced dangerous hairline cracks in the metal of the boilers, making them brittle. '*If you can't drink the water, neither can your engine.*' The railroad foreman's tutorial was still clear in my memory.

What passed for our library was a large, single-roomed clapboard building opposite the clinic and commissary. I picked up the 'O' volume of the Encyclopedia Britannica and read, '*The world's ocean waters contain small soluble amounts of most of the Earth's elements, the largest single item being three and one-half percent sodium chloride salt.*'

That evening while Duano was outside having a smoke, I calculated how much salt I'd need to put into a fifty-five gallon drum of alcohol in order to get a three-and-one-half-percent solution in the final alcohol and water fuel blend. Salting a fuel drum was my best chance of doing the maximum damage to torpedoes at the minimum risk to myself. Twenty-six ounces of salt in a drum of pure alcohol would result in a three-and-one-half-percent salt solution in the fuel mix.

Next, I had to figure how to get the correct quantity of salt into the alcohol efficiently. It had to be premeasured and not conspicuous. Going to our pantry, I picked up the round box of salt on the lower shelf. For once, fate smiled. Right there printed on the label, 'Net Wt. 26 oz. (1 lb. 10 oz.).' The large amount of salt was inconspicuous in its familiar packaging and should appear innocent enough in my possession as part of my lunch—

to accompany my boiled eggs, for example. I would hide my weapon in plain sight.

I joined Duano on the porch. Smelling his cigarette, I took along my pipe and tobacco pouch, readying myself for our nightly smoke and recap of the day. The aroma of my pipe tobacco stood out against the mix of high-tide smells that drifted in from the bay.

Our doors and windows all had interior blackout curtains, making Duano little more than a shadow. His cigarette tip glowed, a small bright spot in the dark. Soon we were engulfed in a cloud of sweet-smelling smoke. A crescent moon provided enough light to keep me from stepping on his foot.

"Did you hear about the big show at the firing dock today?" Duano asked.

Letting the pipe stem drop free from my jaw, I replied, "Nope. What happened?"

"Jesse told me he and Ed rolled out a Mark 14. Jesse sets this fish off and it decides to make a hard right turn, going up onto the beach over on Bainbridge Island. So the retrieval crew follows the trail up the beach and into some guy's front yard. The fish is stuck into the side of his house, still steaming. The guy is pissed about the house, but all he can say is, 'Look what you did to my lawn jockey.' All that's left of the statue is the metal base. The lawn jockey's Black Sambo head is looking up at 'em from the grass, grinning like Al Jolson."

"Wow, I wonder what we get for successful destruction of a lawn jockey?" I asked.

Finishing my pipe, I tapped the ashes out of the bowl as the aroma of Burley tobacco hung in the air. Reentering through the kitchen door, I slid behind our canvas blackout curtain just enough to let me in but no light out.

My supply of eggs sat on the drain-board in a chipped porcelain bowl. Our dozen hens reliably laid one egg each per day. The eggs, rationed now, were our non-regulated bounty, like vegetables from our garden or fish we caught off the ferry pier. I got into the habit of taking two hard-boiled eggs in my lunch as the excuse for having salt in my lunch box.

Mrs. Olson sold the eggs from her own hens, bending the spirit of rationing and national frugality, but no one in our tiny town saw a problem or impolitely mentioned the eggs. Her two dozen eggs usually were gone by close-of-business, so our regular contribution of four eggs became a small credit that we used for beer, tobacco, and other essentials—like salt.

* * *

I had solved the salt dosage problem and the method of getting the salt into the station by early August. It was time for me to get on with winning Bea back by making the government pay for their crimes. I would have twenty-six ounces of salt in the container in my lunch box each day. If challenged about the contents of the salt box, I had enough salt to pour some into my palm for inspection by a guard. Salt kept things simple. While not as efficient for my purpose as acid or even creosote, salt wouldn't arouse suspicion.

Stopping at a small store next to the ferry terminal down the road from Uncle Burt's, I picked up one box of Morton Salt in its blue, pressed-paper cylinder. Morton's bright logo featured a little girl in her rain coat holding an umbrella over her head and carrying the salt cylinder which is accidently spilling out as she walks in the rain. '*When it rains, it pours*,' reads the Morton logo. So I hoped.

I needed to find something that would work as a tool for opening the threaded plug on the head of each fuel drum. Once removed, the plugs were collected in two-gallon buckets. I pocketed one of the plugs as I walked over to find Duano for a lunch break. The nose of my six-inch pliers fit the slotted top of the plugs and would do fine in place of a wrench. Like my choice of salt for a weapon, a well-used pair of pliers in the pocket of a machinist would not arouse any suspicion.

How long would I need to do the deed? I timed the pouring of the salt—full box to empty box in twenty-five seconds. How long to pull the drum-head plug with my pliers? Timing this part of the plan was risky, so I guessed at ten seconds. Thirty-five unobserved seconds with a fuel drum was all I needed to put my plan in motion.

Building 82 was where the delivery trucks off-loaded pallets of fuel drums. The storage area, enclosed for fire safety, had just enough room for a forklift to bring the pallets of full drums down to an open area in the room's northwest corner. Here, the storage area was separated from the fueling floor by a heavy metal fire door.

After fueling, torpedoes were moved outside; they were never unattended as they awaited test firing. Four Marine guards manned a covered machine gun pit. The gun faced out towards the water in anticipation of a Japanese incursion. Two guards faced inward to watch the torpedoes testing.

The blue salt-filled box, a ham sandwich and two boiled eggs filled the bottom of my lunch box, while a glass-lined vacuum bottle of coffee filled the rounded top half. Carrying my lunch onto the station made it subject to random inspection of the contents. This had never happened to me, but two large signs posted on either side of the entry gate boldly stated, '*All persons entering the Pacific Torpedo Station are subject to search of their person(s) and vehicles.*'

I passed through the Main Gate unchecked.

Next were the sentries at the entrance to my own building. Choosing to arrive with six others from my shift, I walked straight into the locker room. Lunch box, jacket, and cap went into my locker. I donned a blue shop coat, took safety glasses from my locker and placed them in my breast pocket before entering the shop floor.

Putting down my grinder at noon, I joined a small exodus of workers who had opted for the first of the two possible lunch breaks. I went back to my locker, changed from shop coat to brown canvas jacket and picked up my black steel lunch box. A small pair of pliers was in my back pocket.

"Pat, you want to join us over at the lunch area by the lagoon?" The call came from Andy Muldow, who worked next to me in the same row of benches.

"No thanks, it's too foggy out there today. I think I'll wander over to 82 and try to catch Duano. If that doesn't work, I'll come looking for you guys."

Walking outside onto Second Street past the Marine guards, I headed over to the west end of Building 82. Duano was the fueling shift crew chief, so he was all around the fuel storage area and at the fueling site itself.

The large metal roll-up door on the west end of the building was open. Stopping near the Marines standing guard at this this door, I was ready for inspection. I knew the guards by sight, if not by name.

"Would you mind if I went in? I'm looking for Duano Lagomarcino. He might be in the fuel storage area, and it would save me going round the corner to the Hunnicutt Road entrance."

"Go ahead. I saw him driving forklift about half an hour ago," the larger of the two guards responded.

"What's in the box?"

Opening the lunch box, I ticked off its contents—ham sandwich, a thermos of coffee, two boiled eggs and salt for the eggs. No matches, no cigarettes, and no bomb. They didn't even look inside, but simply waved me through.

"I can spare an egg if you're hungry?"

"No thanks. Go on in." And I did.

"Duano, it's Pat. Are you in here?"

One of Duano's crew acknowledged me by calling, "He's gone to the locker room. That's where I'm headed. I'll tell him you're out here... unless you want to come along?"

"Thanks. I'll just wait here in case he wants to go eat out by the lagoon."

"No problem. I'll tell him you're over here."

I'd not seen anyone else in the area since I'd come in. I moved out of the direct line of sight of the open roll-up door and the Marines. I rested my lunch box on top of a pallet of fuel drums. Pliers ready and lunch box open, I took out my salt and removed the three-quarter-inch plug from the top of the drum. Sweating now, I poured the salt in and replaced the plug.

The deed done, I didn't feel particularly powerful, yet I no longer felt powerless, either. It had been fifteen months to the day since Bea's good-bye in Seattle, but I'd finally done it!

Duano found me, still sitting on the drum, my eyes closed. Just for a moment I was back with Bea, walking Curley and enjoying ice cream at Shaw's.

I asked myself if I was no longer the kind person Curley had thought I was. If being in doggy heaven enabled him to understand humans, I hoped he knew that I was getting revenge for him.

"Hey, you want to eat or sleep?"

I wanted to eat. And...I wanted to hurt the government again.

16. Keyport, September, 1943

Home from our shifts at Keyport, Duano and I were sitting at our kitchen table. It was a hot afternoon, the first week of September. The heat brought the odor of chicken manure to my nose.

"Listen, I've got a cousin, Giorgio Pelligrini. We grew up together in Jersey. Anyway, Giorgio enlisted in the army in 1940. And in case you were about to ask, that's the US Army, not the Italian army," Duano said, giving me a broad smile.

"Giorgio was a lab tech in a hospital at Atlantic City. The army trained him to be a medic and he was giving shots to recruits at Fort Dix. Close to home, it was a good gig. Last month I heard from my mom that Giorgi got transferred to somewhere out west. I bet you didn't even know that I could read or write, for that matter. Bet you thought I could only trace!"

Another pause and a grin, which I interrupted.

"Get on with it."

"Okay, so I got this letter from Giorgi. I'll read it to you."

August 31, 1943

Dear Duano,

Here I am, up to my ass in sagebrush and jack rabbits. Get out your map and look just south of the Oregon border in northeastern California and see if the towns of Dorris or Newell, California are even on the map. I'm part of a team of medics at the Tule Lake Segregation Camp that the army just took over from the civilian authorities. This is where bad Japs go to die. Us Italians really dodged a bullet when we didn't get locked up like these poor bastards. All told, there are ten internment camps for Japs and then there is us, the one segregation camp. An MP company is here to guard the 'bad Japs' that wouldn't sign our loyalty oath or caused trouble at other camps. We've got two clinics, one outside the wire for the GIs and another clinic inside for the Japs. That's where they've got me working.

Happy trails,

Giorgio

Control of the segregation camp had been taken from the civilian authorities and given to military police. A farm labor strike was given as the reason. The Army immediately set up a prison stockade within the segregation camp. Three hundred and fifty detainees were confined, including Takeo Sakai. Bea's mother had no part in the camp labor unrest but was a no-no who refused to sign the loyalty oath. She was double damned by wanting to repatriate to Japan and her fate sealed by being the wife of a suspected spy.

"Tule Lake never meant anything to me. Except maybe that Giorgio and I might meet up in Portland if we could ever swing leave at the same time. But, I know it means something to you. That's where they put your girl and her family. Yes?"

"Yes," I replied, my attention now fully captured.

"So, I'm thinking maybe Giorgio can contact your girl. Pass a message—you to me, me to Giorgio, and Giorgio to her—while he's taking her blood pressure or passing out aspirin. What do you think? Do you want me to see what I can set up?"

"Yes, please. Yes! Thank you, Duano. Tell your cousin whatever you think he needs to know. See if he's willing to help me. This is great. She's my whole world, Duano, and I've got to get her back."

"See this red stamp and the initials here in the lower left corner. That's from the censor who approved the letter" Duano said as he leaned over towards me and tapped the censors stamp with his finger tip.

"We'll have to be smart with how we go about this."

"I understand, and I'll write Giorgio today. All of us whose last name ends in a vowel are just lucky that we look like everybody else. Bea and the others don't look like us, and that scares the shit out of folks. That's the difference between Mussolini and Hirohito. This is why Giorgio is where he is, instead of being in North Africa. The army can't take the chance of having Italians fighting Italians. It's that simple. I'll let you know what Giorgio can do."

"One more thing," smiled Duano. "This is gonna cost you. I may be easy, but I'm not cheap. If this works, you owe me a beer, maybe two beers."

"Done," I said. He lit a cigarette, and I re-lit my pipe.

* * *

Duano kept his promise and wrote to his cousin. Part of what he wrote after, 'Dear Giorgio,' I had provided. He worked my request into his letter using a code from their boyhood.

September 8, 1943

Dear Giorgio, Do you remember when we worked for Mr. Gladius?

Mr. Gladius, Duano explained, had employed them both as runners in his bookmaking operation. This opening alerted Giorgio that the first letter of each sentence in the next paragraph comprised a name. The hidden communication would remain invisible to the army censor.

Sure those were good times! All the money we made. Kind of miss that now, don't you? About Tule Lake, at least you get to see more than New Jersey. I think the rabbits will be

106

fine, especially with an old fashioned polenta with olive oil and grated cheese.

Leaving the code, Duano completed the message.

Have you seen your old girlfriend Beatrice? I remember that she had the same birthday as my old house number. I played football with her brother Ernie. I heard that he got locked up. Too bad, he was a hell of a half-back! If you hear anything about Bea, let me know. If my pal Pat McBride doesn't find a local girl, I'll pass along her address to him.

* * *

"Hey Pat, I've got a letter from Giorgio. I'm reading between the lines on that. Here's what I got."

September 21, 1943

Greetings Cousin, You asked about my old girlfriend Bea Sanguinetti. I heard from my mom that Bea's teaching at a boarding school, way out in the woods. The school is a dump and she's lonely and misses home. But her health is fine and her brother just enlisted in the Army. Bea's Mom is not so hot. She's confined because of TB and Bea can only visit her once a week.

"That's all I've got for you, Pat. Listen, you write out what you want me to ask and I'll work it into my next letter to Giorgio."

"Thank you for what you're doing, Duano. It sounds like Bea's brother Ernie enlisted in the all-Japanese unit the Army is forming. Maybe that'll take some of the pressure off Bea and her Mom. Anyway, I'll write some notes for you to pass to Giorgio, later tonight."

Those four brief lines woven into the letter seemed a gift beyond price. Bea was away but, just perhaps, not out of reach.

Duano kept up his correspondence with cousin Giorgio. The updates were mostly brief. I'd find letters left on our kitchen table for me. If I wanted something specific from Tule Lake, I'd write my request on the back of the letter.

10/10/43

Hi, Duano,

Greetings from jack rabbit heaven! Turns out that jack rabbits are too skinny and have ticks, so the rabbit stew and polenta idea didn't pan out. Mom says that she saw Bea in person yesterday at her doctor's office. Bea was home from her teaching job. Mom says she's not looking too good. Too thin, no smile. I'm guessing she just needs a man in her life.

Mom did pass along your friend's desire to be a pen pal, and Pat's joke about coming to marry her and getting her out of the woods. She didn't respond to the joke. Mom told her that Pat would bring her a million dollar gift when he came to take her away, but that didn't get a rise out of her either. I don't know what to tell you, but Mom sends her love.

Giorgio

The message was plain. I crumpled the letter into my fist. My love was no closer and seemed to be losing herself.

* * *

Over the coming weeks and months, I repeated my fuel salting at least twice a week. I watched, waited and when the opportunity was there, I acted. Sometimes, I'd find Duano driving the forklift or moving a drum as I walked towards the fuel storage roll-up door. I might wait for him while he went to his locker for his own lunch pail.

The cylinder of salt and two boiled eggs became everyday items in my lunch box. Between the Mercantile, the small store near Uncle Burt's, and stores in Poulsbo and Silverdale, I managed to keep my arsenal supplied without having to hoard such an ordinary item or attract any undue attention by buying it from a single store.

I needed to be able to tell which fuel drums had already been salted. While double salting any drum might produce quicker, more certain or more spectacular results, it would also be more suspicious. I noticed that each drum had been marked with its reception date, written in yellow grease pencil on the drum head. Yellow grease pencils were common to every building, if not every worker. A grease pencil on my person would arouse no suspicion. My marking of drums had to fit in with the real marking system and without raising any suspicion. In the end I decided to put a simple checkmark next to the date on those drums that I'd already spiked with salt.

At home, I burned the empty paper salt boxes in the trash burner compartment of the Wedgewood stove in our kitchen. I lifted off the black metal lid on the stove top, inserted the empty salt cylinder to nestle amid dirty paper napkins, and then lit the trash with a wooden kitchen match.

My fear of being caught lessened with each act until, magically, I no longer had any fear. The heat of the flames warmed my hand through the beige porcelain sides of the stove. When I finally lifted the metal burner lid to clean the ash drawer below, the smell of the burned paper trash met me and covered over the aroma of stale burnt coffee. In the grate above the ash drawer were thirty-six small tin pour-spouts that had survived the flames. I dumped the lot into the out-house in the yard.

With twenty-seven torpedo runs poisoned by each contaminated drum, I may have sabotaged hundreds of torpedoes. I knew from our bulletin board that each completed torpedo represented a ten-thousand-dollar investment for the Navy. Was it enough for me that I might have cost the government millions of dollars? Probably not, but I had done something. I was squaring the debt that the government owed me and the Sakai family. Just how much damage the invisible corrosion did to the metal of the turbines, I never knew.

* * *

It was Halloween of 1943 before we heard back from Giorgio.

Hello from jack rabbit heaven! I've been trying to come up with a way to help your buddy get his lady out of the woods and into his arms. This is tough, even with all the reasons that he has. I'm not sure that even ten thousand reasons would be enough. I've not given up. If I figure out how I can help play cupid, I'll let you know. Sorry. Mom says hello.

17.   Keyport, 1943

Keyport, Washington was the final assembly and distribution point for the Pacific Fleet's torpedoes. Above Keyport in the Bureau of Ordnance structure was Newport, Rhode Island. The Newport Naval Torpedo Station, founded in 1869, was our parent and—in their own estimation—our better. They were the 'think tank' and creators of experimental new designs. Until the late 1930's, Newport built all the torpedoes for the Navy, and each was virtually hand-made. By 1939, the Navy began looking into ways to get the larger number of weapons they knew would be needed. The answer lay in harnessing American industry to mass-produce components for the needed weapons. These components were shipped to assembly plants on opposite coasts: to Alexandria, Virginia and to Keyport, Washington.

American Can Company sent us torpedo body-housing sections. Hudson Car Company shipped us bronze turbine engine castings. The Singer Sewing Machine Company made air flasks and fuel tanks. If we could just manage not to 'screw up' Newport's good work, the Navy and its vastly expanded need for torpedoes would all be fine. So said Newport to the Navy.

A wood pier jutted out one hundred yards into Liberty Bay on the southeast corner of the torpedo station. The pier was the terminus of a narrow-gauge rail track that moved finished torpedoes from the final assembly shop to be test-fired from the end of the pier. At the end of the pier, Ed and Jesse, the launch supervisors, met the bronze giants. The pier was one of my favorite spots to escape our building for a break or during lunch. Watching the goings-on and listening to the torpedo testing crew gave me insight into what I was a party to building.

The crew slid the torpedo into the firing tube at the end of the dock. The firing tube was then lowered fifteen feet down into the water. The launch supervisor pushed a button, sending a blast of compressed air into the rear of the torpedo firing tube, and the steam-powered monster was forced out into the water. Once released, the inner workings of the torpedo sent it on its way. A mist of water and alcohol fueled the turbine engine and generated the steam that propelled the weapon through the water. The two spinning fans of the turbine raced to twelve thousand RPM's in less than half a second as a steady supply of steam was produced by the twelve-hundred-degree fire. The turbine drove the torpedo ahead at forty-six knots. The force of the steam, once beyond the two spinning turbine blades, vented out the rear of the torpedo as a harmless trail of bubbles.

The torpedo would simply float after the propellant was gone. After three successful test firings, each separated by a complete disassembly and inspection, the finished torpedoes were fueled and armed with an explosive-filled warhead. Lacking only detonators, they left Keyport to be shipped to submarine squadrons in Hawaii and Australia.

The submariners, now at war in both oceans, began complaining loudly and constantly about persistent problems of duds and premature detonations by the Mark 14 torpedoes. These reports filtered up through the submarine fleets to the highest levels of the Navy. Newport believed the complaints received from the Navy to be self-serving excuses from inept captains, or the overblown exaggerations of a few anomalous events. Newport convinced the Navy that there were no real problems. Later, when the reports of problems persisted, Newport claimed that the torpedo assemblers were to blame.

I learned, years later, that Newport had never tested the torpedo depth control setting gauges they had produced. The Newport gauges made the torpedoes run eleven feet too deep.

Newport's new magnetic exploders didn't work because of a materials issue. The aluminum firing pin assembly had design defects that turned many direct hits into duds because the firing pin bent on impact. These two problems, long denied by Newport, hurt the effectiveness of our submarines and the morale of their crews and gave cover to my attempts at sabotage.

After the battles of the Coral Sea and Midway Island, America had only two functioning aircraft carriers. So the Pacific submarine squadrons remained our country's main defense against Japan in 1942 and 1943. In the shadow of Newport's denial of its own role in the Mark 14 failures, I had found a means to my desired end. Their own hubris would give me cover to gain revenge on the government. I was in no hurry to take my vengeance. The knowledge of my plans made the waiting tolerable. While perfecting turbine blades with my tools, I was simultaneously exacting retribution.

* * *

By the late fall there was still a steady stream of complaints about the many problems with the Mark 14s. In response to long-standing grievances from the two Pacific submarine squadrons, Newport sent a team of engineers and senior production staff to Keyport.

Arriving just after Halloween, 1943, the seven-man inspection squad bent to their task of setting our work right. The two engineers on the team—one a mechanical engineer and the other a metallurgist—managed to self-identify by wearing new blue knee-length shop coats. The two senior production staff wore more functional denim shop aprons. The two outliers turned out to be representatives from parts suppliers. Hudson Motors, which cast the turbines that I worked on, and Mack Truck Inc., which produced the torpedo driveshafts and planetary gear assemblies, each had its own man on the team. Heading the team was the Newport torpedo production team representative.

Escorted by their own sets of Marine Guards, the seven— sometimes individually, sometimes in pairs, sometimes all together—would turn up anywhere in the station. They observed different operations, sometimes conspicuously close, almost leaning over our shoulders. They were neither polite nor rude—asking occasional questions, always getting and never giving information. They were there and then they were gone without a word. Their behavior and silence were unnerving, but I was able to keep my own discomfort well hidden. For almost two weeks, they visited the shops, fuel storage, assembly and storage buildings. They also spent long hours carefully observing the test firings.

Tuesday afternoon as I worked at my bench, a group of approaching figures in my peripheral vision caused me to look up. Coming down the aisle between the rows of lathes and work benches were Capt. Olson, two of the visitors and two Marines.

We had nicknamed the visitors Manny, Moe, Jack, Larry, Curley and Shemp. The leader of the invaders from Newport was dubbed Herr Doktor, based on his projected disdain for everyone at Keyport. The names fit the inspectors based on some particular physical attribute, such as facial hair, glasses, body type or haircut.

Manny with the glasses and Larry with his bushy hair were in tow. Olson was in the lead and spoke for the group.

"Pat, we'd like to talk with you. Can you come along with us?"

The combination of the two inquisitors and the two Marines walking behind Olson was a chilling sight.

I spoke not a word. Had I been undone by some small detail? Was there an artifact of the metal that provoked an "ah-ha" moment from the chief inquisitor? I'd have to brass it out.

The words I expected to hear ran through my mind. *We know you sabotaged the torpedoes. What do you have to say for yourself?*

I put down my grinder and followed Olson outside. Walking toward our unknown destination, I had denied myself the small comfort of a jacket. The cold and damp of the season fit perfectly with the mood of our little parade.

We rounded the corner of a building and entered through a guarded door. Down a flight of stairs, I followed Olson through double doors into a brightly lit room. Inside were the other four inquisitors—Moe, Jack, Curley, Shemp and Herr Doktor. The door closed behind us. The Marines remained outside.

None of these cream puffs are capable of beating a confession out of me...well, Captain Olson, maybe, I thought to myself. What came to my mind next was Uncle Burt and Juan de Fuca—Wanda Fuca, and how he had fooled me into believing him. You can sell the lie with a straight face. This lesson that I'd learned years ago might get me through this inquiry— or not. I hoped none of them noticed the sweat that was oozing down my side and darkening the armpits area of my shirt. It was the captain who broke the silence.

"Pat, we want you to look at some recovered turbine parts and tell us what you see." He pointed to a collection of turbine castings and blades that lay on the table top. "These parts represent what we've found in three Mark 14s that died in the water. We'd like your opinion about what you see in the metal. We're trying to find the cause of these new problems we've been seeing over the last two months."

All eyes were on me as I slowly examined each of the recovered parts. I saw blades that had shattered, and turbine housings that had cracked from the twin strains of heat and acceleration. The bronze surfaces appeared clean, though slightly tinted by shimmering blue rainbows of heat and the orange patina of corrosion. I was smiling inside now, so I waited to answer. The more parts I fondled, the more my audience anticipated my words. Suddenly, it dawned on me I was being offered a place at the right hand of the inquisitors. They wanted my help! Finally, in my most professorial tone, I started to speak.

"Captain, I'm just a line worker, a glorified machinist. I'm not sure I'm your man."

"Pat, you are just the man we want, because you see these turbine parts every day. Both of your supervisors tell me you are

115

the most skilled grinder in the building. These gentlemen know a lot, but they don't have the practical, day-to-day experience that you do. We're hoping you can see something in these failed parts that they aren't seeing."

Half turning his head toward Herr Doktor and his group, Olson added, "Our subs are having far too many problems with the Mark 14, and we don't have any alternatives, so we need to figure it out. Besides the problems with hits not exploding and sure shots missing, now we are getting reports of torpedoes dying in the water."

"There may be design problems," I suggested, while seeming to study the failed parts.

Herr Doktor sniffed loudly and looked away from me.

"Have you been able to tell from the torpedo serial numbers if this new problem is taking place with all the Mark 14 torpedoes or just the ones assembled at Keyport?" I was poking at Herr Doktor with each question—and I enjoyed it more than I probably should have.

"Only on Keyport torpedoes," offered Herr Doktor.

"It looks to me like you either have a problem with the alloying of the bronze castings, or else sea water is getting into the turbines somehow."

They didn't even feel it when I set the hook and started to reel them in.

"Maybe there are small leaks in the torpedo skins. If there are no signs of leaks, then maybe a momentary vacuum is being created and a little water is back-flowing into the turbine when the fuel is expended. That would be an indication of a design flaw in the torpedo."

This was just plain fun now. The responses I saw on four of the faces clearly read as "couldn't be." If there was a vacuum problem, Herr Doktor would have no one to blame but himself.

"The failures I'm seeing are not just with the blades but also with the turbine bodies. The preparing of the bodies, the preparing of the blades, and the assembly of the turbines are all done by different work stations. This rules out either sabotage or plain sloppy work."

I set my jaw and chose to enjoy the moments of silence that followed.

"Add to that the fact that this new problem of unexplained torpedo failure is isolated to Keyport, and is not happening at Alexandria, I think that what we have here is a bad batch of bronze castings from Hudson."

Moe winced at my conclusion.

Then Herr Doktor fixed his gaze on Moe, who stuck an index finger in his shirt collar and started to rotate his head from side to side.

"They might not even have realized the problem if the metal billets that Hudson received from the foundry had been alloyed incorrectly. Hudson wouldn't necessarily know the metal was bad and it would make all the difference in the durability of the turbine blades." I felt a little bit guilty and hoped this would be believed because I liked Moe and wanted to get him off the hook. He was not one of the Newport assholes. I hoped that Moe hadn't shit his pants.

"Mr. McBride, we appreciate your observations and...opinions. I'm sorry we had to pull you off the job in such a hush-hush way, but we needed your assistance on a confidential basis. Please."

Herr Doktor seemed to put a little more emphasis on pronouncing *opinions*, but I could not deny him this small sanctuary. The inspection team now spoke among themselves in low but animated voices, while completely ignoring me, as apparently I had served my purpose. Breaking in, Olson motioned me toward the doors.

"Thanks, Pat. I knew you would have some ideas."

Gesturing with a nod toward the knot of inquisitors, he finished his thought as we passed through the doors.

"Even if the Newport egg-heads didn't want to hear it, they still needed your help. They don't know shit from Shinola about what we do. The guy in charge, according to my counterpart at Alexandria, they call "Wade the Blade." The only thing that he wants to fix is blame. I would consider it a personal favor if you would keep this meeting just between us though."

"No problem Captain. I'm glad to help and flattered that you chose to ask me. Can I head back to my bench now?"

"Sure Pat. Thanks." He offered a smile and a handshake as I left.

As I walked out, I savored the sights and sounds of freedom, and the sweet revenge of my small victory.

"Yup, probably a design flaw," I repeated, to no one in particular.

Newport was still unwilling to either own their design mistakes or to admit that Keyport was turning out a good product. Whether they hung their hat on an unknown saboteur or some lazy cabal of slovenly workers, Newport remained certain that the fault didn't reside with them.

* * *

Newport's other attempt to find a scapegoat to blame for their malfunctioning Mark 14 torpedoes involved searching for a saboteur. Agent Brigham Young Belknap of the FBI was tasked with finding out if the Keyport torpedoes were being sabotaged. Agent Belknap was looking for me, although he never knew it. And despite the damage I had managed to do, Newport's own failures were the real culprits most of the time.

Lacking any skills that would allow him to realistically fit into some part of the Keyport production team, Belknap had been introduced as an efficiency expert. He could plausibly be in any part of the station observing and evaluating operations. I'd seen him in his blue shop coat, clipboard in hand, loitering around Building 73.

Belknap had not spoken to me, nor had I seen him speak to anyone else. I caught him watching me one afternoon, standing behind me. I'd felt his presence and stepping back from my bench, I bumped into him.

His 6-foot 5-inch frame had enabled him to stare over 6-foot me. I looked him up and down. His spit-shined brown shoes and brown slacks were visible below the shop coat. A white shirt and tie showed above his coat collar.

"Sorry pal, didn't mean to crowd you. I've been watching you for a while now." Raising the clipboard in a gesture of its significance, he added, "efficiency expert," and smiled.

"Tell me about what you're doing," he said as he gestured toward the turbine blades on my bench. He listened with apparent interest as I briefly explained my job and how the turbine blades were the beating heart of a torpedo. Apparently satisfied with my responses, his smiled momentarily broadened and he said, "Thanks."

Turning to leave, he looked down and stared at the bronze dust that now showed like glitter on the shiny polish of his brown shoes. He wasn't moving, so I offered him a red shop rag from my pocket. I watched as he meticulously wiped the metal dust from his shoes. I recalled seeing such shoes in the Cinnabar. After wiping the metal dust from the toes of his shoes, he passed the rag back, nodded a thank you.

"I'll try not to step on you next time," I said as he headed back toward our locker room door.

* * *

Three nights later I answered a firm knocking at my back door. Lifting the blanket blackout curtain I saw Chief Olson and a tall stranger standing outside in the dark. I stepped aside, held the door open and the blanket folded back, inviting them inside.

119

The tall stranger spoke first. Olson's companion was the efficiency expert from the shop.

"You lent me the rag to wipe my shoes?"

I nodded in agreement.

"Special Agent Belknap," he said as our prolonged handshake ended. I gestured to our kitchen table, inviting them to sit.

This was business and Chief Olson came right to the point. "Pat, Newport still believes the torpedo problems the submarine fleets are complaining about must be due to something going on here," Olson explained. "Carelessness, laziness, a spy in our midst or nothing at all, we need to know which. Agent Belknap has been playing the part of an efficiency expert from private industry, hired to make recommendations about speeding up production. But what happens is that his very presence in a work area causes people to change their behavior,"

"Mr. McBride, thanks for meeting with me. I've been poking around Keyport for months and frankly I'm wasting my time. I've also been hanging around bars in Poulsbo and Silverdale where torpedo station employees drink. I nurse a beer and listen to conversations. I'm neither a machinist nor an engineer, but I'll know what I'm looking for when I see or hear it, if that makes any sense," Belknap said, with just the hint a smile. "So far I've found nothing and I'm hoping you might have some suggestions for a new approach."

Olson waited for the agent to finish before continuing.

"He's working alone and doesn't have months and months to get embedded in our operation. Do you have any suggestions about how he could see without being seen?"

I needed to think of ways to give Belknap enough access to satisfy Newport while keeping him away from my clandestine work. Until that moment, I had no idea how lucky I'd been not to have been discovered during Belknap's first two months on the job. I'd probably dodged a literal bullet. Finally it was my turn to speak.

"This is pretty far removed from anything I've ever done, Captain. So remember my advice is probably worth little more than what you're paying for it—which is nothing.

I turned to Belknap. "As the captain may have told you, I was asked to look at metal parts from failed torpedoes. What I saw made me think the Mark 14s have inherent design problems or we get defective parts. I know that Newport doesn't agree, but I've not changed my opinion. But you're asking for my help to catch a potential spy, not my opinion as a master machinist, so I'll try to be objective here.

"I see that we can't have you on any of the shop floors. Obviously, nothing is going to happen while you're lurking around, efficiency expert or not. What I would do is put you up on the roof with binoculars, so you could watch the shop floors undetected. I know my building has a clerestory for light, and I'm guessing most, if not all of our buildings have some sort of skylight or window that would work as an observation point. Just like deer hunting...get to a good spot, sit still and keep your eyes open. Captain, you'd have to arrange that with the Marine garrison commander so Agent Belknap doesn't get arrested or shot. Tell him that your man here is inspecting roofs or something, and don't mention anything else."

"Good idea," said Olson, nodding to Belknap who nodded back before I spoke again.

"Oh, and lose the suit. You need to dress like a working man. Get some work clothes and a clipboard. Hide your binoculars inside a lunch box. Better yet, if the glasses are small enough, fit them into your coat pocket.

"I think trying to overhear idle chatter in the bars is a good one. Buy a few rounds. Loosen some tongues and nobody questions a free drink, even from a stranger. Worse case, they think you're queer. But they'll probably take the free drinks anyway."

Olson and Belknap looked at one another, but neither word nor gesture was exchanged.

"I appreciate the suggestions," Belknap gave an approving nod. "They make a lot of sense in terms of my going unnoticed, yet still having the opportunity to see what I need to see. Please keep my presence here confidential."

"No problem," I replied, still not believing my luck.

"Okay, we're done here. Thanks again. If we need more ideas or a change in plans, I'll let you know," said the captain as he leaned across his kitchen table to shake my hand.

Then I shook the agent's hand and wished him good luck with as much sincerity as I could fake. Once they were out of hearing range, my feelings erupted into words.

"I hope you fall off the roof and break your neck, you FBI asshole."

Now I needed to see if there were skylights in the fueling storage area. I'd just never looked, but now I would. I didn't plan to stop taking my revenge.

There turned out to be a clerestory above the fuel storage area, too. Before attempting to salt any fuel drums while Agent Belknap was around, I'd first make sure I had located his stake-out spot for the day. Although he was smart enough to find a spot, lie down and watch quietly, ladders leaning against a building were his tell. I also learned which buildings had metal ladders permanently attached to allow easy access.

Number 82, where I salted the fuel drums, was one such building. This made it harder to pinpoint his spot. If I couldn't locate Belknap's surveillance spot, my salt box just stayed unopened until the next time.

I never got called back for another skull session with Olson and Belknap. Agent Belknap skulked around on various roofs for another month. He bought a lot of drinks in all the bars and drank a lot of 7Up, but never found a culprit at Keyport responsible for the Mark 14 torpedo failures.

* * *

The rap on our door came three times.

"I'll get it," sighed Duano, pulling himself up from his chair. "Pat, it's Captain Olson, for you."

"Invite him in, Duano."

"He wants you to step out on the porch." When I did step out, we shook hands and turned our backs to the door.

"I'm sorry for pulling you out of a warm house. I just need a minute," said the chief of security.

"No problem," I replied, stuffing my hands into my pockets while otherwise ignoring the chill.

"Agent Belknap has moved on. He did find some problems through his surveillance efforts. A dope peddler, a loan shark and a ring that was stealing gasoline. He's turned these cases over to me. What he didn't find was any nest of spies, saboteurs, slackers or other irregularities that could impact our torpedo production. He'll report back to his superiors and they'll pass it along to Newport, the Navy and the Bureau of Ordnance."

"That's good, I guess. Newport seemed hell bent on pinning their problems on us. I'm glad they couldn't do it."

"Well, you helped the bureau before, so I owed you Belknap's final report. Thanks Pat. Now, I'm going back to my own warm kitchen."

"Thanks for the info. Regards to your wife, Captain," and we shook hands again before going our separate ways.

18.   Keyport, December, 1943

Christmas Day, 1943, fell on a Saturday, but we worked anyway. War doesn't honor holidays any more than it honors human life. Andy had been invited to dinner with his landlords. Duano and I had plans to catch the 5 p.m. bus into Poulsbo. We'd have Christmas dinner at Einar's Kitchen, the best restaurant in town.

Greeting us at the door with a smile and a handshake, Einar pulled us inside. Dinner was Einar's Special—no menus, the food served family style. The place smelled unlike any restaurant I knew. By the end of our relaxed dinner I could match the exotic smells with the equally unfamiliar dishes. The aromas of pickled herring, lutefisk, and Aquavit had become familiar. Our evening schedule was shaped by having to take the 11 p.m. bus that took the graveyard shift workers to Keyport.

We waited for the bus, still full and warm from our meal at Einar's. The bus stop was large, with a bench and wooden cover that protected us from the falling snow. While we talked and waited, a single car moved down the block, its headlights mostly obscured by blue paint. It moved in our direction, wheels quieted by a flurry of snow. Lost in our conversation, neither of us noticed the car slow and angle into the bus stop. Suddenly the amber Pontiac emblem was plowing headlong into Duano, just missing me. Duano bounced off the hood. The car struck one of the posts that supported the shingled roof of the bus shelter. The roof fell, striking a glancing blow to the car's windshield and passenger door, as the heavy sedan slid to a halt.

"Duano! Duano!" I yelled and rushed around the wreckage. Crawling under the remains of the shelter roof, I saw Duano lying on the sidewalk, wincing in pain.

Between barrages of swearing, he said, "I think my leg is broken, and my hip hurts. Good thing I'm drunk, or I'd really be hurting."

Patrons and restaurant staff had come out of Einar's by now. Einar himself came running out close behind them.

"I've already called the cops and asked for an ambulance. They'll be here pretty quick. Let's move him inside until they get here. Can someone check on the driver?"

Einar and I moved around behind Duano. I kept up a conversation, hoping to keep his mind off the pain.

"Hey, we don't want to lift you, but we think it's not going to hurt so much if we just gently reach under your arms and drag you. Okay, we're going to lift just a little and if you don't yip in pain, we'll pull you out and over across the sidewalk to the restaurant."

Einar and I grabbed him gently, and not getting any moans or curses from Duano, we pulled straight back toward the building. Then we dragged him down the block to Einar's. Inside on the linoleum floor, the snow on the back of Duano's coat and pant legs began to melt.

Kneeling at his shoulders, I turned when the small bell hanging from the doorframe tinkled. Two men I knew only from dinner entered with a third man supported between their arms, his head drooping to his chest.

"Driver seems to be okay. He was passed out in the seat."

"Sit him in a chair over there," said Einar.

"I oughta beat the shit out of..." then Einar paused in mid-sentence. "Or maybe not. He's an Army officer. He probably has a reason for being drunk."

As they carefully placed him in a chair, I noticed for the first time the driver wore an Army uniform. The volatile smell of whiskey rolled off his uniform and skin. He was 1st Lt. Robbins of the Army Air Corps, according to his name badge and insignias. Above his left breast pocket were two rows of decorations, among them the red-and-blue ribbon that I knew to be the Distinguished Service Cross. He was hatless, with traces of snow starting to melt down his face. I wondered what memories, secrets or sins Lt. Robbins needed to drown in alcohol.

"I'm dead," Robbins mumbled over and over, all the time his head rolling side to side as if keeping time with a silent tune.

"I'm dead. I'm already dead. I'm so dead," continued his litany.

Two other diners who had been helping came back inside.

"We turned off the car and set the brake. Keys are still in the ignition. The cops who just arrived said the ambulance should be along any time now. Can we help with anything else before we take off?"

"You fellas come back and have a meal on me. Thanks an awful lot," Einar said.

The drunk shifted his torso, his head lolling back and his mouth hanging open.

A white Cadillac ambulance with a large red cross on the door arrived at the crash site. The police pointed the two attendants with the gurney toward Einar's. I edged out the door until I had eye contact with the ambulance crew and waved them in. Holding the door open, I gave them a quick briefing.

"He says his leg feels broken and his hip hurts."

Looking up from the floor, Duano winced. "Merry Christmas, guys."

"Where's he going?" I asked the attendant at the head of the rolling gurney.

"We'll take him to our hospital here in town. How's the other guy?" asked the attendant.

"Screw him," was Duano's response.

"Stinko drunk, but otherwise he's okay as far as we can tell. I'll go check in with the cops and make sure they know he's here," I said.

The attendants loaded Duano onto the gurney, covered him with a blue wool blanket and left for the hospital. I walked outside to where the police cars sat. I introduced myself and explained the driver that hit Duano was drunk and asleep inside Einar's. One officer made notes in a small brown leather notebook as I recounted the accident from my perspective.

My interviewer said his partner would see to getting the drunk driver to the station, and he'd be glad to give me a ride to the hospital in the meantime. He'd also get us back to Keyport after Duano got out, if needed.

"My brother-in-law, Charlie, is the chief of security at the station. He's not Norwegian, but still not a bad sort—for a Swede, I mean."

"He's our landlord. Duano and I have the little house behind the store. They're real nice folks. We've been there since February of 1940. Small world, huh?"

The drive to the hospital was brief and uneventful.

"Listen, you go in and see how your friend is doing. My name is Phil. When you get things settled, have Nola—the night shift charge-nurse—call me at the station. Then I'll come over and drive you home."

"It's good to meet you, Phil. And thanks so much for the lift."

I sat in a waiting room where walls, floor and furniture were all a uniform beige, and the smell of disinfectant hung in the air. Duano was being examined by a petite female doctor.

"You have a clean break in your right femur. The hip is just sprained and should feel better in about a week. The leg we're going to cast in a minute, here. I'm going to give you some Darvon with codeine to take now and for the next couple of days until the pain subsides. You should be fine, but you'll be off your feet for about six weeks until the cast is removed. Sorry that your Christmas had to end like this. Your friend can have some coffee while we get you fixed up."

Turning to me, she directed me to the waiting room. "He'll be done and ready to go in about an hour—once the plaster has a chance to set."

"Thanks, Doc," I said.

I must have dozed off in the waiting room. Nurse Nola's gentle shaking of my shoulder woke me without giving me a start.

"Your friend is ready to go. We safety-pinned his slacks back together as best we could, but I don't think he'll be worried about modesty much...at least not tonight. The Darvon has kicked in pretty good, so he'll sleep, mostly. My husband will be back in a few minutes to drive you both to Keyport."

"Thank you. I really appreciate the help," I said, truly grateful for the kindness and care we'd received at the hospital.

"You're welcome. Anyway, we'll send everything over to the Keyport station clinic. Phil already phoned the news of the accident to the night duty officer at the Keyport Security Office, so they know you may not make it to work tomorrow. The doctor would rather not keep him in the hospital here. She likes to keep beds open for any overflow from the Naval Hospital at Bremerton, just in case."

I nodded and mumbled, "Thanks again," as Officer Phil came through the blackout doors into the emergency room waiting area. Duano was rolled out in a wheelchair. His cast, which extended from ankle to upper thigh, was held up by a raised footrest on the chair, sticking out at a right angle like a plaster battering ram. A white surgical sock covered his bare toes against the cold.

I pushed Duano's wheelchair out while Phil held first one door and then the other. Arriving at the car, I reached under Duano's legs and slid him, butt-first, into the back seat. Duano's back was pressed against the door, his cast extending across the back seat and his crutches lay on the floor as we drove back to Keyport.

When we arrived home, Phil helped me get Duano into bed.

"I gotta pee," Duano informed us.

I thanked Phil and sent him on his way, then retrieved the crutches from the porch and found Duano a pint Mason jar for a urinal.

"Here, use one of these."

"I'm gonna need a bigger jar than that."

Placing a quart jar on his nightstand and the crutches next to the head of the bed, I asked, "Need anything before I go to sleep?"

Duano simply shook his head, then nodded and sleepily smiled his appreciation.

"Get some sleep, paisano. I'll see you in the morning."

* * *

When I awoke late the next morning, I knew some coffee and scrambled eggs would go a long way to help us get over the late and crazy night. As I divided the eggs onto two plates, I heard the first stirrings from Duano's room.

"Lazarus, is that you rising from the dead?"

Duano appeared in the doorway on his crutches.

"Good morning. Thanks for getting me home and all, last night."

A knock at our back door interrupted us as Duano fell awkwardly into a kitchen chair. Captain Olson waited at the door.

"Good morning, sir. Come on in. There's fresh coffee if you've got the time."

"Thanks." He stepped inside and spoke to Duano.

"Poulsbo Police phoned me about the accident. The fella who hit you is back at McCord Field, and his commander has been advised of what happened. I've informed your building chiefs that you'll be gone for a couple of weeks. You're on paid medical leave, so there'll be no interruption in your pay. Your prescription has been transferred to the pharmacy at Poulsbo and they'll send the drugs over here. We'll let Pat know when a script shows up at the station clinic and he can bring it home for you."

Duano nodded that he understood.

Turning to me, Olson asked about my status.

"Pat, are you going to make it in today or do you need to be here?"

"I'll be in later after we eat. I'll see what needs to be moved so the wounded warrior here can get around."

Turning to Duano, the captain offered his hand.

"Well, I'm sure glad to hear that the leg is going to be fine."

Catching my eye, Olson signaled with a small turn of his head that he wanted a private word with me, so I followed him out.

With only the two of us on the porch, Olson whispered to me.

"The guy that hit your friend is Donald Robbins. He was Colin Kelly's co-pilot. The Army has asked that we make last night's events go away. I wanted you to know, because I could use your help getting Duano to let it go."

"Wasn't Kelly the pilot of the B-17 that was supposed to have blown up a Jap battleship in Manila Bay on December 10th 1941, before he died in the plane crash?"

Olson nodded.

"Only Kelly didn't sink a battleship in his attack, he got shot down instead."

"So the whole bomb dropping down the smokestack of the battleship story—that didn't really happen?"

Olson nodded again. "The public needed to feel we were striking back. Actually, Kelly's plane was damaged by a Jap fighter. The crew bailed out, but Kelly's chute didn't open. The rest of the crew, except Robbins, was captured by the Japanese. Robbins turning up alive now would be bad for the war effort and an embarrassment to the Army, given the story that was initially put out," whispered Olson, holding my gaze.

"No problem," I said, heading back inside.

I understood the chief's need for my help, and I understood the country's need for a hero on the heels of Pearl Harbor. I understood why Robbins drank, too. He had to keep the secret. He was not the person on the inside that the outside world believed him to be. The lie was forced upon him, and he had to live with it every day. I understood perfectly.

Back inside, I passed coffee and a plate of eggs to Duano.

"I think that just letting go of last night is the best thing for all concerned. I understand that the guy who hit you is real sorry and is probably in deep shit with his commanding officer already. Can you just let it go?"

Without hesitation, Duano replied.

"Sure. That'll be my Christmas present to him."

"I'll take care of the chickens and bring home a paper after shift. When I make my lunch each day, I'll make double so there will always be a sandwich left for you to eat at noon, and coffee on the stove. I'll get a bucket for you as a chamber pot until you can hobble out back."

"Forget the bucket. I'll get myself to the outhouse if it kills me. If you could, maybe get some boards and lay down a path from here to there so my feet don't slip or my crutches get stuck in the mud. That's all I need."

"Sure, I'll take care of that before I go in today. There's a pile of old boards alongside the store that will work. If you don't get tired of my cooking or break your neck getting to the crapper and back, we'll make this work until you're back on both feet."

My breakfast finished, I cleared my dishes to the sink and spoke over my shoulder.

"So, how do you feel, anyway?"

"The hip hurts worse than the leg this morning. I'll be fine, especially if I wash down the pain pills with a little bourbon."

I reached into a cabinet, took down the bourbon, and set the bottle on the drain board.

"Tap her light on the bourbon while you're taking those pills, Duano. I'm gonna grab those boards, then head into work. Is there anything else you need before I go?"

Duano shook his head as he ate, his crutches lying on the floor at his side.

Heading out the door, I spoke over my shoulder.

"I'll see if I can get you a visiting nurse. What's your poison, a blonde or redhead?"

"Blonde, please. Oh, I almost forgot, can you get my jacket and cigarettes from my locker? The locker key is on my key ring in on my dresser."

"Done," I said, as I emerged from his room and closed the door to leave the house.

* * *

Walking over to Building 73, I knew I was about to lose access to the fuel drums. My sabotage was not yet complete. If I was going to strike again, now was my best—if not my only—chance.

When noon arrived, I got my lunch box from my locker and headed toward Building 82. My choice of entry points would depend on who I found on guard duty at the doors. Outside the open roll-up door to the fuel storage area were two Marines I didn't recognize, so I continued on to the locker room. Two more strangers guarded this door, but trusting my own planning, I continued. Showing my ID badge to the sentries, I smiled and spoke.

"I came to get my roommate's stuff from his locker. He's Duano Lagomarcino, head of the day-shift fueling crew, and he's home on crutches with a broken leg. May I go in?"

Looking from my face to my badge, then back to my face, the Marine corporal shook his head. The stink of stale cigarettes coming from his uniform made my eyes water.

"Your badge doesn't allow you access to this building, Mr. McBride. Sorry."

"Would you be willing to see if you can find either the Bureau of Ordnance supervisor or the officer-in-charge? I'll stand right here if you'd see if you can locate one or the other of them."

The Corporal paused a moment, then spoke to the other guard.

"Private, go see if you can find one of the building supervisors while we wait here."

"I heard about your friend. I'll check your lunch box while we wait."

I opened the box and held it out for inspection. The sentry lifted out the sandwich, eggs and salt, checking for anything in the bottom of the box. Returning the sandwich and eggs into the box, he opened the spout on the salt cylinder and poured a small amount into his hand. This guard was being thorough, but I had confidence in my routine. He tasted the crystals and spat. Returning the salt to my lunch box, he extracted the thermos. He unscrewed the bright metal top that served as a cup and then unscrewed the top of the vacuum bottle. Steam rose out of the opening up into his face and we both smelled the enticing aroma of hot coffee. Satisfied, he resealed the thermos and returned the bottle to the lunch box. The salt, my weapon, had aroused no suspicion, there in plain sight.

We waited in silence. Soon, the familiar face of the ordnance supervisor appeared from inside the doorway, followed by the Marine who had fetched him. Seeing me, he smiled.

"How's Duano?"

"A pain in the ass—so, about like always. He's in a cast and on crutches for six weeks. He asked me to retrieve his jacket and smokes from his locker. Can you help me with that?"

Looking to the Corporal, he said, "I'll take Pat in. No problem, Corporal."

I followed the supervisor into the locker room and waited while he checked a clipboard list of locker assignments. Steam from an adjoining shower room humidified the air, dampening the imbedded smells of dirty bodies and dirtier socks. Finding Duano's name, he pointed to the last bank of lockers on our right.

"Number 129. Have you got the key?"

I extracted the key from my pocket and held it up for his view. We went to the locker and removed the brown canvas jacket and a partial carton of cigarettes.

"Thanks, can you get me out through the fuel storage area? I'd like to see if any of Duano's crew is there, so I can fill them in."

"Sure, that's no problem. Listen, I've got to hit the latrine, you know the way, so I'll catch up with you there."

Crossing through the fueling area, I saw two members of Duano's fueling crew. I kept walking, but gave them a quick status report on Duano as I passed by.

Alone in the fuel storage area, I looked around and, seeing no one, called out a hello. Getting no response, I moved to a pallet of fuel drums and began my practiced routine—lunch box down on a drum head, open box, remove salt and pour. I had to keep my eyes on my pouring so as not to leave any telltale salt on the drum head, so I was always nervous while I poured. The sound of footsteps in the storage area made me look up. I saw the ordnance supervisor coming my way. The salt box in my hand went back into the lunchbox.

"Pat, what are you doing?"

I stopped breathing. The supervisor's expression was blank while he waited for my answer. *Think, think, think!*

"I keep dropping the cigarettes from the open carton we got from Duano's locker, so I'm trying to put the packs inside my lunch box to get them home." My heart raced, but I kept eye contact and held up the open cigarette carton.

"Okay, get them loaded up. I'll walk you out past the sentries."

I loaded the cigarette packs into my lunch box and closed the lid. My heart rate finally began to slow. Taking Duano's canvas jacket under one arm, I walked with the supervisor out to the roll-up door. He took the empty carton from my hand.

"Tell Duano to take care. We'll see him in six weeks."

When I strolled past the sentry post the guards took no notice of me. I guess their job was to keep saboteurs from getting in, not from getting out. I was sweating under my jacket as I walked to the lunch area. I knew that I had just barely escaped getting caught. I didn't like the feeling, and decided at that moment to wait for Duano's return before attempting another attack.

A new and worrying thought suddenly came to mind. If my sabotage was discovered, Duano could get blamed. We were at war with Italy, after all. Never mind that Italian-Americans hadn't been singled out and imprisoned like Japanese-Americans. Fuel that was under Duano's control had been the instrument of my revenge. If it ever came to Duano being accused of my crime, what would I do? This new realization troubled me. Duano was my friend and not some soulless part of the government. I walked back home unsure of the future of my planned revenge.

19.   Keyport, Winter, 1943-44

What to do from so far away? I had no car to cross a thousand miles. If I ran to Bea, we'd still be fences apart. Then I wondered; could I buy her way out? I turned the idea over and over, polishing it and trying to see each of its facets, like the diamond I thought it could be if I squeezed this lump of coal hard enough. I needed to share my notion with Duano and, if he didn't laugh at the idea, see if Giorgio would help.

I started my list on loose-leaf paper:

1) Have Mom send my money from home.

2) Find Bea a safe place, outside of the West Coast Military Exclusion Zone. Ask Margie.

3) Give Bea a new identity with a believable past that explains her lack of identification.

4) Price to get her out? Getting her a travel ticket and cash?

5) Help from Duano and Giorgio?

Acting upon the urgency that I sensed in Giorgio's letter, I began. The first letter was to my mom.

Mom,

I'd like to move my money to a local bank up here. Please cash out my account at B of A.

Love, Pat.

My second letter was to Mrs. Alex McLaren, the former Margie Watanabe. Margie was feisty and protective of Bea. I asked if she had any friends or relatives living anywhere out of the exclusion zone who might be willing to take Bea, should she be out of Tule Lake. I didn't hint at how Bea's release might happen.

I found Duano out smoking on the porch and explained to him the key elements of my plan.

"Would you be willing to see what Giorgio thinks of my idea?"

"Sure, I can ask. He might say no, but that will be up to him," Duano replied.

"Listen Duano, if the plan is too risky for you or Giorgio, I understand, and I'll find my own ways. No hard feelings."

His answer came out after a long silence.

"An Italian helping a Japanese-American seems only right somehow. How much of an incentive are we talking about?"

"Between the money in California and what I can have, say two months from now, $4,000."

"How about this—I'll loan you another thousand. That makes for a more attractive number. I'll have it whenever you need it. Now, I got to tell you...this worries me, Pat. Bad things, good things, they're all mixed up here. Remember how we swapped stories about our dads?"

I nodded, recalling how the darker shades of the lives of our dads had helped form our friendship. Duano continued fixing me with his gaze.

"We had this Uncle Max. Now, I never met Uncle Max, but I know that Max had a mink farm up in Minnesota. Pop sent him a check every month. So, finally I asked Pop about Uncle Max. All that Pop would say was this, 'Son, if you ever have to do something bad, do it yourself. Never hire it out, because if you do, you've got a partner for life!'" Then Duano stared off into space, thinking.

"If we go with your plan, then you've got a partner. I'm solid. Giorgio is solid, and you are solid, too. But now you've got a crooked guard as a partner for life. And I guarantee you that he isn't doing the Lord's work. He'll be participating for the worst possible reason—money. Just know that going in."

"Understood," was all I said.

"Now, let me get to work on a letter to Giorgio. I'm also going to tell him to see if he can get a post office box somewhere nearby. We'll need it down the road, if we're sending money or anything else to Giorgio that can't be inside a letter that's censored. We'll try to get something set up in case we need it."

An hour later, Duano interrupted my pipe smoking with his proposed note.

"Listen to this and tell me if it works."

Dear Giorgio. How are all your rabbits?

"Then there's a paragraph of family bullshit before we get to the main item. Here it is."

My friend Pat really wants to take Bea out of the woods. He's given me five thousand reasons why she should come away with him and I'm tired of listening. If you know anyone who could help her, I'll have him send his reasons on paper for you to see.

He's hoping that you can locate a guide that would be willing to shepherd her through the woods. Pat's hoping that the thousands of trees in that particular forest would give her cover from any bad weather, until she got back to town. Pat's working on a new job for her, somewhere with friends, until he comes to pop the question. Giorgio, Pat's a romantic jerk, but he's my pal. I'd appreciate anything you can do.

I was remembering Cal Newell. Do you remember him, big guy that was the bag man for Mr. Gladius? Great guy! Each day he had a donut for us. Thoughtful, he was. People don't seem to be that nice anymore. Or, maybe the world is just not as nice anymore. Before when we were kids, the donut was a big deal. Orange frosted donuts were always my favorite. Exactly like my Aunt Sally used to make.

Regards to your mom.

Duano

Duano was brilliant. His 'Mr. Gladius' code asked Giorgio to get a PO Box. I guessed that the code had no words starting with 'X,' so 'Exactly' would be understood in context.

"This is beautiful, Duano. Don't change a thing. I'll mail it tomorrow."

The letter went out the next day. While I waited, I thought about how to get Bea from outside the camp to her safe harbor. The fourth leg of my plan lagged, but could not be perfected until I got some good news from Margie.

My mom's letter with a cashier's check for $4,032.28 arrived Nov. 14. Margie McLaren's letter came one week later.

Dear Pat,

Alex has a sister in Muscatine, Iowa. He says that she's willing to help, to a point. We need to come up with a believable family connection for Bea. My sister-in-law, Hazel, has visited us and met my folks, so I can't pull a sister out of thin air. Hazel's husband is serving in Europe. I've never gotten the feeling that she is a racist at all. She has accepted me into the family with no problem. But there is a clear line in her thinking about our enemies, especially with Brad being overseas. Being a sister-in-law, I happen to be on the right side of the line. My best idea is for Alex to introduce Bea as Mrs. Patrick McBride. Remember when the three of us were in Seattle and you kidded Bea about being an Eskimo? Hazel can be told that Bea is from Alaska! She looks the part, and if we make her not a

Japanese-American, she'll be a lot more acceptable to Hazel and other folks in the Midwest.

Lots of details, I know, but what you're proposing is not some kid running away from home. This would be serious business for us all. I'm racking my brain for an explanation of why Mrs. McBride would need to stay in Iowa and not here in Stockton, San Bruno or Seattle.

Bea has stopped writing and just seemed so unhappy, so crushed by all of her family's suffering when she last wrote. I know you miss her desperately, and I'm worried about her too. Let me know what you decide to do and your ideas on how we could justify Iowa. Let me know what you think of my idea.

Love, Margie

I went over the details with Duano.

"Margie is right about needing a reason for Bea to go to Iowa instead of California or up here." The validity of the "Why Iowa?" question was clear in my mind.

"How about this? She has to go to Iowa because there is no housing for our families at Keyport. In places like Seattle, San Bruno or Stockton she gets mistaken for Japanese," suggested Duano.

"I like it. It's simple and partially true—always the best basis for a good lie. You're smarter than you look, you know that?"

"Fooled you, didn't I? And you thought I was just a pretty face," Duano joked.

"Believe me, Duano, I never thought that. Not for a minute."

A ring was no problem. If Bea McBride, a girl from Alaska, was introduced as a newlywed whose husband was away serving, no one would blink. She didn't drive so lack of a driver's license fit. The newly created Social Security cards hadn't been issued to residents of the territories like they had for the states. Having no identification was no longer such a problem because she was being vouched for by the McLarens. I kept polishing the plan in my mind as I waited on the other elements of it to come together—primarily Giorgio's help, costs and transportation.

20.   Keyport, January, 1944

I brought in our mail and handed two envelopes to Duano. He read both, showing me a get-well card his mother had sent. While reading the second letter, he asked me to bring him a pencil and paper.

"It's from Giorgio, and there's a private message."

January 20, 1944
Dear Duano,
I got a letter from our old boss Mr. Gladius...

"Give me a minute to figure out the message."

I sat quietly and waited.

"Okay, here's what you got.

"Crooked guard, needs double fee for transport out to KFO. Use POB 10, Newell."

The message, like most of real life, was a trade-off for my hopes. There was a way out, but at a price I couldn't meet, at least not yet. We figured that KFO stood for Klamath Falls, Oregon, and that Post Office Box No. 10 at Newell, California, was Giorgio's. More good news, Klamath Falls is both a train and bus stop, so it would be easier for me to get to, and for her to leave.

I sat down with Duano to finalize a plan.

"Ask Giorgio to make this offer to the guard. I'll come up with the $10,000 somehow. I want him to get Bea a bus ticket from Klamath Falls to Muscatine, Iowa. He has to put her on the bus with a suitcase of women's clothes. I'll also send traveling money for her, a wedding ring, and a letter with details about where to go, whom to see and her cover story. If he'll do all that, then I'll pay the full $10,000."

"Okay, suppose he does go along with the new deal and will do these last few things— the bus ticket, clothes and traveling money. How are you going to come up with the extra cash?"

"I got the $4,032 from my bank. I've been saving all I could from my pay, so I've got another $800 now, and the $1,000 that I'm getting from you. So, I've got over $5,800 right now. I'll come up with something to get the rest. I just have to."

Duano tilted his head forward.

"Look, I can come up with another thousand. And I know a guy back home who could get the rest. There'll be some interest, what we call 'vig,' on what you borrow, but it can be done."

"Thanks," I said, speechless. Maybe I should have said more, but I could find no words to express how grateful I was to Duano for getting me over this hurdle.

"Have Giorgio tell the guy that if he agrees, I'll send him half now and pay the other half when I get word that Bea has arrived in Iowa."

"I'll do it, and we'll see what he says."

My problem was not solved, but my plan had advanced. Two weeks to the day and I had my answer in a letter from Giorgio.

Tell your pal that his 10,000 reasons worked, and the specials were fine too. Send your promise now, inside the travel book you had been reading, and I'll read it and share it with my friend. It will probably take about three or four weeks to finish the book, so any travel will be done about then. The guide works part-time as a mail clerk, so he'll keep an eye out for the book. Regards to your mom.
Giorgio

I put $5,000 in $100 bills in the pages of a thick book, wrapped it in brown paper and tied it with string. I hollowed out a space in the pages and placed a plain gold wedding band in the improvised compartment. Under the brown paper wrapping, I taped a letter to Bea inside the book's cover. The letter was concise in its instructions. It provided an overview of our plan, her new name and a cover story. Fifty dollars traveling money was also enclosed. She was now to be Beatrice Ghgaan-Kagani McBride, formerly of Sitka, Alaska. Her father was a Tlingit Alaskan native, and her mother an ethnic Chinese. Whoever was helping me on the inside must have access to incoming mail before it was examined so my special package would not alert the Army.

"Where'd you come up with the name?" Duano asked.

"It means 'light of the sun,' I read it in a book," I answered.

My letter to Bea included the address of Alex McLaren's sister where she could stay until she got her own place. I told her to write me, in care of Margie. The envelope instructed the guard to give it and the enclosed ring to Bea. Duano put the book in the mail to the box Giorgio had rented.

21.   Keyport, February, 1944.

As I worked at my bench, the background of machine noise in Building 73 made me unaware that Bill Glasscock was standing two feet behind me until he tapped me on the shoulder. Setting down my grinder, I let the safety glasses fall from the bridge of my nose with a flick of my right index finger. When I took one step back, Bill spoke into my ear to be heard above the factory din.

"Pat, Commander Munson would like to see you in Building No. 1 after shift."

"Okay," I said.

Arkansas Andy on my left also got called over and a message put in his ear. Nodding that he understood the instruction, Andy turned back to his work. Moving down the line, I stepped over to Andy's bench and leaned into his ear.

"Munson's after the shift?"

He signified "yes" with a nod rather than a word.

Seeing Commander Munson—let alone being told to report to his office—was not an ordinary event.

"Something's up, but I have no idea what."

"It's probably those good-conduct medals we've been expecting."

He smiled broadly, and I grinned in response.

After shift, Andy and I walked up the hill to Munson's office. Entering the building, I spoke to one of the two Marines guarding the small lobby,

"Which way to Commander Munson's office?"

"Straight ahead, up the stairs one flight. Take the hallway on your right, and his office is in the right-hand corner."

The guard gestured straight up with his thumb, signifying that we were standing directly underneath Munson's office.

"Thanks," we said, and proceeded up the stairs.

We turned into the right-hand hall where a small group of men lined the wall outside the commander's open office door. We walked to the end of the line. I recognized some of my co-workers—mostly grinders like me. I stood next to Charlie Hanford.

"You have to check in with the commander's receptionist. Then she'll send you back here to wait. Munson's supposed to arrive in about five minutes."

The receptionist looked up from her desk, checked our names off a list and repeated what Charlie had said. We returned to lean against the wall and wait. There must have been a back entrance to the office because the receptionist responded to an intercom buzz.

"Yes, commander." Then she spoke to all of us standing out in the hall. "Commander Munson is ready for you. Please go in and have a seat."

Andy and I followed Charlie into a conference room. A long wood table with what must have been two dozen heavy wooden chairs filled the center of the room. Our number filled all the available chairs and left me, Andy and Charlie standing against the wall.

Commander Munson stood with his back to a chalk board. Lying on the table was an assortment of theater-size posters. The posters were from defense contractors, each touting the company's contribution to the war effort.

Cadillac—In the Vanguard of the Invasion

The poster showed endless waves of the P-38 Lightnings providing air cover to troops and tanks assaulting a beach.

The Lightning, the P-40 and the Mustang—powered by Allison.

America's foremost liquid-cooled aircraft engines all carry Cadillac-built parts.

In land invasions, Cadillac-built tanks are often the first to hit the beach.

Motor Car Division—General Motors Corporation

My eye was drawn to the Fairbanks-Morse poster, done all in shades of gray, depicting a submarine returning to safe harbor with a broom tied to its highest mast. Above the sub, in bold white lettering, was *"CLEAN SWEEP."* Opposite the quote was the image of a Western Union telegram.

Fairbanks-Morse Co., Beloit, Wisconsin. Diesel engines of your manufacture powered the USS Wahoo in her recent spectacular victories off Northern New Guinea. The Wahoo sank a Japanese destroyer and two days later sent to the bottom a four-ship convoy consisting of two freighters, a transport loaded with troops, and a tanker. For this magnificent effort, the Wahoo today wears a broom on her conning tower—the Navy's traditional decoration denoting a "Clean Sweep." You who furnished her fine diesels share in this honor. Keep 'em coming! R.L. Cochran, Rear Admiral USN.

Commander Munson cleared his throat to get our attention and the group went silent.

"Gentlemen, 1942 and 1943 were tough years for us. Our enemies have mostly had their way so far, but now the tide has started to turn. Thanks to our brave men and women in uniform, and thanks to all of you here at home who provide them the weapons to fight and win this war. Moving into 1944, we are making more weapons and better weapons than ever before. Newport's recent efforts have focused on our next generation— electric torpedoes that will be free of the Mark 14s tell-tale trail of bubbles. Those bubbles have served as a clear line-of-sight back to our submarine's location, putting the boats at risk from counter-attacking patrol vessels. In 1943, we recovered from a Virginia beach, a German electric torpedo that had missed its target. The work of our scientists, coupled with their reverse engineering of the German machine, gave us a working electric torpedo, identified as the Mark 18. Next month, Keyport will be switching over from production of Mark 14 steam powered torpedoes to the new Mark 18 electrics. Our changeover will affect us all, but you men most particularly. The country still needs you, however. There is still a long war to be fought and won. But you'll be leaving Keyport."

Inside my head, I repeated Munson's words. *Next month, we'll be switching from production of Mark 14 torpedoes to the new Mark 18s.* My sabotage was over. Between Duano's injuries, which had cost me access to the fuel drums, and my nearly disastrous attempt to act without Duano as cover, I was ready to stop. No more Mark 14 steam torpedoes being produced at Keyport cinched the end of my plan. Munson paused and turned to Commander Stillman, the senior representative for the Bureau of Ordinance at Keyport, who had been standing quietly in the corner of the room.

"Thank you, Commander Munson. We want to give each of you men a choice of where you'd like to work next. As you leave, Mrs. Black will give you a list of openings. The list contains both government jobs and key spots in private industry where there are defense contractors that need your special skills. Look over the list and decide what we can arrange for you. Your pay, benefits, and draft exemption will all remain in place if you choose to stay with some branch of the government, or key contractors involved in the war effort. Please make your choice within the next week. Give your signed election form to the ordnance supervisor in your building. On behalf of the Bureau of Ordnance, I want to thank you all for your service to date and in the future."

Nothing more was said and we looked around at one another. Mrs. Black had moved from her desk to the conference room door, a stack of pages in the crook of her right arm. Waiting for the table to empty as the others filed out, I looked at the posters until Andy nudged my elbow. Exiting, we passed through the veil of her lilac perfume and each took a single page from her hand.

"Time to go."

Once down the stairs and through the lobby, our group idled between the headquarters building and the main gate. We made our way to our various destinations—some to the bus for Poulsbo or Silverdale, others to the ferry pier or down the hill to their shifts.

I was at peace with what I had done and thinking about stopping my campaign of revenge. Fate—in the form of a drunk driver, nearly being caught in the act and a captured electric torpedo —had made the decision for me.

"Got time for coffee before your bus?" I asked Andy.

"Sure. That'd be nice. Thanks."

We took a table by the side window facing the ferry dock. We each looked over the page of options we had been given. Andy immediately voiced his selection of McAlister, Oklahoma. The ammunition plant at McAlister was close to Andy's home in Hot Springs, and had been his original job site of choice.

"What looks good to you, Pat? My choice was easy."

Looking over the 30 options, I saw lots of aircraft jobs— Martin, Hughes, Douglas, Boeing and Northrup. I looked over ammunition plants—Longview, Texas; Springfield, Missouri; Harper's Ferry, West Virginia; and Andy's choice, McAlister, Oklahoma. I could go to a tank factory in Michigan or, if I had a strong stomach, to Newport, Rhode Island, and work on an antisubmarine weapons project. Recalling the Fairbanks-Morse poster on the conference room table, I saw diesel submarine engines as a means to stay closer to the railroad. I was familiar with the Fairbanks-Morse opposed piston, or OP, diesels as we called them at the rail yard in San Francisco. But their plant in Beloit, Wisconsin, was even farther away from my home. Continuing down the list, I saw Mare Island Naval Shipyard in Vallejo, California. They needed people to install the four OP diesel engines that were put in every newly launched sub. Vallejo was in the Bay area.

"Mare Island Naval Shipyard, Vallejo, California," I said firmly.

This was the job for me for whatever time I had left in government work before resuming my life with the railroad after the war. This choice would keep me close to the rails, advance my skills, and give me the all-important opportunity to visit Bea when I traveled back to California. I looked forward to our reunion.

I'd have to break the news of my departure to Duano tonight. His leg had mended, and with a straight face he was telling young, unsuspecting girls who asked about his limp how he'd been "wounded in action."

Stopping at the mercantile, I got us two quarts of beer. I put the beers in the refrigerator while I waited for Duano to arrive home from his shift. I was smoking my pipe outside on our porch as he came into view, halfway between the main gate and the mercantile.

"Can you manage a beer?"

"Absolutely."

I went inside for the beers, then handed one over to him.

"Rainier beer—ah yes, the good stuff!"

"You mean, the only stuff?"

"That, too," I said, taking a pull. "Hey Duano, I've got news, but it's sensitive, so don't talk it around."

"Let me think. This being Valentine's Day, you're going to tell me that you are a woman trapped in the body of a man, and you just can't fight it anymore? You're going back to California, the land of fruits and nuts. Am I right?"

"Besides that," I said. "Today they called about 15 of us into Commander Munson's office. Keyport is going to retool to make the new Mark 18 electric torpedoes, and stop building Mark 14s. I'm out of a job. Andy Muldrow and Charlie Hanford are in the same boat, along with some guys from Building 94. They gave us choices of where we'd like to go."

Drawing the list from my shirt pocket, I passed it to him. Duano eyeballed the paper in silence.

"I think I'd like to go back to something closer to the railroad. That's where I'll be anyway, after the war. The best choice for me seems to be the Naval Shipyard at Vallejo, just across the bay from San Francisco. They're building subs there. The OP diesels that go into the boats are used in our diesel locomotives. Working with the new diesels will put me in good shape when I leave the Bureau of Ordnance after the war."

I held out my brown quart and we clinked bottle necks in a toast.

"Good for you. Congratulations. Is this a for-sure deal or do you have to apply?"

"My placement request has to be approved by the bureau. But, I'm pretty sure I'll have a lock on the job because of my good work here and my background with the railroad."

Leaning forward slightly and lowering my voice, I continued.

"I can see Bea on my way home. I'll be getting a job that will set us both up after the war. She's had it rough, and I know that this will be the good news she's been waiting for. She may even be in Iowa by the time I get out of there."

Left unsaid was how I expected my great secret—the sabotaged torpedoes, the million dollars in blood-money that they represented—to show my loyalty to Bea and result in restarting our lives together again.

Duano smiled broadly.

"Good for you. Good for the both of you. I've seen how you worry about her, even though you try to hide it."

"In case you haven't thought of it, electric torpedoes don't need fuel, so you'll be getting a new assignment too," I replied, as a means to stop him from going on about something that I knew had a second face. I was not proud of what I had done—nor was I ashamed—but I couldn't share my secret with Duano.

"Wow, that's right. I hadn't thought of that," said Duano, a pensive note in his voice.

"You'll be fine. You've got good skills that will always be needed by lots of shops on the station, so don't worry."

He lit a cigarette as he spoke.

"How soon?"

"It sounds like the transition to the Mark 18 will be in about a month. We'll finish work on the Mark 14s in the pipeline now, but I expect to be gone by mid-March. I'll be giving Commander Stillman my choice on the new job tomorrow."

The next day I handed my signed selection list to Bill Glasscock, the Bureau of Ordnance supervisor in my building. Opening the folded sheet, he looked at my selection.

"I know you came to us from the railroad, so I think this is a great choice for you."

On the following Monday, I was finishing the final polish on the blades of a turbine rotor when Bill came to my bench and passed me an envelope. He leaned into my ear to be heard above the noise of the shop.

"Pat, here's the word that's come down from the bureau. You got the job at Mare Island. You'll be lead man installing the four diesel engines that go in each of the new Balao class subs."

"Thanks for all your help," I said back to Glasscock.

"I hear the Balao subs are the new big boys—four hundred feet long, five thousand horse power, and carrying twenty-six of our torpedoes. Congratulations. You'll still be doing important work, but for the Bureau of Ships instead of the Bureau of Ordnance. They are allowing you one week of paid travel leave. Here's a voucher, Keyport to Vallejo. See the travel office and they'll fix you up with a ticket."

"Bill, if it can be arranged, I'd like to see my folks before reporting for work. I'm not sure if I'll be getting a travel voucher for the train, the bus, or what...but if that comes up when you see the commander, would you pass along that request?"

Left unsaid was my plan to try and see Bea at Tule Lake.

"Thanks. I really appreciate your help so that I can visit my folks on the way to Vallejo." I shook Bill's hand as I spoke.

Bill broke off the handshake with a back-slap.

"Your reporting date to Mare Island is March 13. Mare Island's Housing Office will have a billet arranged for you when you arrive. You can stay where they put you or find your own place if you prefer. Okay then, that would mean your last day here will be Friday, March 3—in just over a week. Not much time to get ready, so if you need a weekday off to arrange transportation, I'll take care of it. You just let me know."

I walked over to Andy's bench after Bill left. I filled him in and got a thumbs-up and a wink in acknowledgment. Later that day, Andy got his visit from Bill as well. He'd be departing for McAlister on March 9, and had the same basic travel deal that I got, so he could be home in Hot Springs before reporting to the new job. I cupped my hands to yell over the background noise.

"A beer after shift?" I asked.

"Absolutely, we need to celebrate," smiled Andy.

I knew I would miss Duano and Andy, but not as much as I wanted to shut off my memory of Keyport and my secret. I wanted two things now: Bea and peace of mind. Walking up Second Street as our shift departed, Duano caught us as he headed home from his shift.

"We're going for beer. Want to join us? We have news."

"From your smiles, it must be good. Are you two good-news boys buying the beer?"

"I'll buy the beers and meet you guys at the ferry dock," I said.

The open space of the dock seemed a better fit for my mood than sitting on our porch. The three of us walked up the small grade and out the main gate, lunch boxes in hand.

I bought six quarts of Rainier—probably more beer than we could drink, but the occasion made me want to at least make the effort

We walked out to the end of the pier. When Andy popped off the three crown caps, the aromas of hops and malt greeted us even before our first sips. Our bottles clinked together in a toast. Between long pulls on the beer, I filled Duano in on my news and Andy followed with his.

"Fruits and nuts. I knew it," Duano smiled.

It was good to have some friends to share my news. With Duano not included in the relocation offer, we figured he would likely continue as a forklift driver or the like somewhere on the station. I told Duano that the meager furnishings we had collected were all his to keep. We planned our final dinner for Friday.

"We need to talk, back at the house," I said to Duano.

Once back home, I told Duano I'd need some point of contact, like a phone number if possible, for Giorgio and/or my unknown inside man.

"I can reach you through the phone at the mercantile, and leave a message through Mrs. Olson. I'll pay what's-his-name or Giorgio—whatever they decide—when I go through Klamath Falls on my way home. Not much time for this all to come together before I hit the road for Mare Island."

"I'll pass your departure date to Giorgio, and get you some way to contact Giorgio or the other guy. If you're lucky, she'll be gone to Iowa by the time you get to Klamath Falls. Maybe you two can meet for coffee at the bus station," he kidded.

22. Tule Lake, February, 1944

It was 4 p.m., and Bea had finished her work day in the camp school. Outside the air was thick with blowing dust and the tang of sage from the ubiquitous brush that covered the high desert. Among the 11,000 detainees in the camp were several hundred children. Innocents themselves, they had been tainted because of their parents. She was still at her desk when the military police corporal came in. Under his arm was a book, and a night stick adorned his belt.

"Are you Beatrice Sakai, No. 82308300, daughter of Taeko Sakai?" asked the MP.

"Yes."

"Your mother is sick. I'm to bring you to her in the close-confinement unit. Get your coat and follow me."

Collecting her coat, Bea followed across the housing area inside the wire fences and into the cement-block close-confinement building.

She followed him quietly past two guard stations. Her escort, not needing to speak, simply nodded to each set of jail guards and was passed through to the building's interior. She followed him into an empty hallway and obediently stopped while he unlocked a cell door and motioned for her to enter. The cell was empty. A steel bed frame hung off the wall and a small combination toilet and sink occupied the rear corner behind the bed platform.

"Sit down. You might as well be comfortable," the soldier directed.

"I'd rather stand," she replied, avoiding eye contact.

"No, you wouldn't," the MP said, as he pushed her into a sitting position and closed the cell door.

"Where is my mother?" Bea demanded, in an angry voice.

Her voice was silenced by the force of a hard backhand slap that caught her chin and cheek. She tasted blood as her lip began to bleed.

"Now princess, keep your mouth shut and listen."

Opening the book he carried, the MP began to show off its hidden contents.

"This is a letter to you from your Pat. He had arranged your rescue. However, too bad for you both, I was supposed to be it."

He put the letter into his khaki jacket pocket. Fanning out paper money, he continued.

"This is the money he paid me to get you out."

He folded the bills and they disappeared into his trouser pocket.

"Ah, last but not least," he said, holding up the plain gold band before dropping that into his pocket as well.

Bea looked on without speaking.

"Now for the best part," said the soldier. "This letter is my insurance that you and your Pat will never rat me out." He spit the final sentence into her face as he leaned down.

"Because your Pat, in trying to get you out, has become a traitor to his country!"

He stood straight and lifted her chin with the palm of his hand.

"I've decided that you are going to provide a little bonus for me."

Bea slapped his hand away.

"Feisty! I like that. No wonder he was willing to pay me so much. You are going to service me."

"Never," was her response through clenched teeth.

He smiled down on her.

"Some Jap bitch is going to drain my pipes. Would you rather have it be your mother? She's old and pretty dried up, but I'm betting her mouth is still warm and wet."

His threat was clear.

"Get down on your knees," his voice low and smooth, thinking there was no need to command anymore.

She knelt on the cold concrete floor. He held himself, flapping his penis across her face in blunt slaps until she opened her mouth. His hands came hard and fast to the corners of her mouth, his thumbs pushing her cheeks in at the back of her jaws. She tried to recoil from the pain the pinching and stretching brought.

"This little trick is so I don't get bit."

Tilting her head up, he entered her and forced himself to the back of her throat. Bea tasted blood as her teeth tore the inside of her cheeks.

"Lips, it's all about the lips," he said.

Bea began to gag as he pushed against the back of her mouth. Blood and saliva mixed and dripped onto her dress.

"Here, let me help you," he said, as he began to force her head back and forth.

She gagged, her eyes tearing and overflowing. Blood ran from the outside of her cheek beneath one of the thumbs that pinioned her jaw.

When he was done, one of his hands moved to the top of Bea's head, holding her on her knees. Reaching for her hair, he used it to wipe himself off.

Gasping for breath, Bea vomited on the floor, soiling her dress and flecking his shoes. The bitter smell of stomach acid and puke assaulted his nose.

"Hey!" he slapped her. "Clean up this goddamn mess."

He held out a roll of paper that had been sitting at the toilet and sink. "Wipe it up and flush it down the crapper."

As they walked back through the guard post and into the main compound, the sharp smell of stomach acid lingered in their noses. The assault focused all the hurts and damage that white America had done to her family into one. Now she was done with any idea of rejoining anyone or anything in this bastard society.

"Remember your mother," he said as he walked off.

23.   Keyport, March, 1944

I began looking at maps to check my options among train and bus routes from Seattle to Tule Lake. The camp had a Newell, California, address, but that little town was on neither a state highway nor a bus route. The travel office was open, and my 9:10 a.m. arrival put me third in line. I surveyed one of several maps, some showing rail lines. The one in front of me, according to its legend, was The National Greyhound Bus Route Map. Dorris, California, on Highway 97, was the nearest town I could reach by bus or train.

"Next, please."

Looking over my shoulder, I saw the middle-aged clerk smiling and motioning me over. "Good morning. I'm being transferred to Mare Island at Vallejo, California." I handed over my voucher.

"I'd like to depart on Saturday, March 4. My reporting date at Mare Island is March 13. If possible, I'd like to visit my aunt in Klamath Falls on the way down. My family lives in San Bruno, just south of San Francisco. If you can do it, I'd like to go by bus and be routed through Klamath Falls to San Bruno."

"Let me see what we can do for you. If you go the way you want, you'll be responsible for any extra charge—that will not be at government expense. Understood?"

"Understood."

Going to the "Fares and Routes Directory," she noted down a fare, plus departure and arrival times.

"You can leave Keyport on March 4 on the 9 a.m. ferry to Seattle. In Seattle, you'll connect to the noon Greyhound Express bus to Klamath Falls, Oregon, that will arrive at noon on March 5. You can get off in Klamath Falls, see your aunt and get on the next bus. The bus from Klamath Falls to San Francisco runs daily. You'll leave from Klamath Falls at 6 p.m. and arrive in San Francisco at 8 a.m. the next morning, then take the commuter bus to San Bruno. That costs you $12 more than the allowed fare from Keyport to Vallejo. Will that work for you?"

"Yes ma'am. That will be just fine. Thank you for helping me out with the routing."

"Here you go, young man."

Taking the ticket from her hand, I thanked her again for being so helpful and passed $12 across the counter. All of my plans were falling into line. I'd finally be able to show Bea that I was not part of her family's destruction. Sharing my secret would win her back.

* * *

Duano was feeding the chickens when I got back to our house. I poured myself a cup of coffee and sat down at the kitchen table to make a list of what I need to accomplish during my last week in Keyport. I had to square things with my landlord. I leaned out our back door and asked, "Duano, you want to keep this place when I leave, right?"

"Sure, absolutely," his response came above the excited chicken noises from around his feet.

"Okay. I'll check with Mrs. Olson today and let the housing office know on Monday that you want to stay and will need a new housemate."

Duano nodded and walked into the henhouse to collect today's batch of eggs.

I'd have some payroll or maybe personnel records to take with me to Mare Island. I'd have to turn in my security badge before I left the station. This place had given me no peace, but it had given me the opportunity to settle a score. I would never remember Keyport fondly: just that I got even.

I saw Mrs. Olson later that day and told her about my pending departure. She volunteered to have her husband, Charlie, inform the housing office of the vacancy for a single man, starting Monday, March 5. My rent was already paid through February and she told me not to worry about the four days in March.

"You've been a good tenant and will be missed, Pat."

I thanked Mrs. Olson for her generosity and for volunteering Charlie's help.

Arriving on Monday for my last week of work, I found that Ray Majeski already knew about my departure as well as Andy's.

"Congratulations on the new job! Do a good job on those new boats. The Balao and the Mark 18s are gonna help our fleet a lot."

"The supervisor told me I could pick up my records at Building No. 1 any time after 2 p.m. Friday. I'll need to stop at finance, personnel and the security office to turn in my badge."

Ray reminded me to empty my locker and grab any of my own tools that might be at my bench.

Word of our departures had made it clear around the building. I started getting handshakes and good luck wishes from co-workers. The man they thought they knew was getting a warm send-off.

Duano and I made daily stops at Smith's Café after our shift for coffee and to check for a letter from Giorgio. When the letter finally arrived Duano read it and passed it over to me.

Duano,

If you ever do get leave, don't come here. Tule Lake is the drizzling shits. But, if you did show up here, you could ask for me with the sergeant of the guard at the main gate to the camp. They'll find me at the clinic or contact me at my barracks. If he's around, I'll introduce you to my pal who has the book. He says thanks. The school teacher is still in the woods, but I think she'll be gone by my birthday. Bring me some torpedo juice if you ever come through.

Giorgio.

"Duano, when is his birthday?"

"March 3."

My final days on the job passed quickly. Returning from lunch on Friday along the test-firing pier, I decided to clean out my locker and make my way up to collect my records. Andy and Charlie had the same idea and were emptying their lockers, too. As we finished, Ray Majeski and Bill Glasscock walked off the work floor into the locker room. Looking at the three of us, Ray spoke.

"Come over here, please, all of you. I have a decoration to honor your service here at Keyport."

"I was a submariner in the Polish Navy. You had to be tough to be in our submarine service, because all our submarines had screen doors. I escaped by boat to Denmark and then made my way to France. I volunteered to fight the Germans, and those arrogant assholes told me that Polish help was not needed to defend France. Then those cheese-eating surrender-monkeys folded like a cheap paper fan. I and some other Polish officers made it to England. I was commissioned into the British Navy, and later received a lateral transfer into your Navy. "

Reaching into a plain brown paper lunch bag, he withdrew three faux decorations. Dangling from wide red ribbons were miniature torpedoes, the size of cigarettes. Placing one ribbon over each of our heads, he solemnly presented the awards with a speech.

"This is the highest honor of the Free Polish Navy—The Order of the Torpedo Fish. It signifies that you would have been too full of shit to float, except for your also being full of hot air. Thank you for your service."

Ray saluted us.

I was surprised that receiving this thanks from Ray, even paired with his joking, made me feel sad and almost regret what I had done to harm the torpedoes—almost. Getting the unexpected thanks from Ray and feeling his sincerity and appreciation was powerful stuff.

The three of us turned in our ID badges as a final act before departing. Capt. Olson himself was at the security desk to shake our hands and receive the badges. After I handed over my ID card, he handed me an envelope.

"Inside is a letter to the station commander at Mare Island Naval Shipyard. The two paragraphs introduce you as a valued worker who will be missed by all at Keyport. Pat, there is a specific reference to your having been a consultant for Newport. It summarizes your record and vouches for your attention to detail. It's signed by Commander Munson, Commander Stillman, and by me."

He had envelopes for Andy and Charlie as well.

Waiting for the dinner hour, I packed my pigskin bag. Left out were my shaving kit and traveling clothes. Among my possessions was an address book with names and addresses of friends I'd made around Keyport. I'd had a good-bye dinner with my Uncle Burt and cleaned up my room, not wanting to leave a mess for Duano. Then I fed the chickens, whose eggs had served me well...in so many ways.

One last simple dinner—three guys with three steaks seated by the window in the only diner in Keyport. It was absolutely forgettable in all respects, except that it represented the end of a chapter in my life. I came away from Keyport with "friends-for-life" from Trenton, New Jersey, and Hot Springs, Arkansas. My greatest gift to them both was to keep my secret to myself.

24.   Enroute, March, 1944

My suitcase sat by the front door with a jacket draped over the top. Duano and I shared coffee and a final breakfast of toast and eggs until it was time to leave. I had my jacket and hat on and was reaching for my suitcase when Duano intervened.

"Let me."

We walked the two blocks to the ferry dock. Looking up at the gray sky, I shared my thoughts.

"I won't miss the gray and the damp, that's for sure. I owe you much, Duano, including a standing offer to visit me after the war."

"Here," said Duano, placing an envelope in my hand.

I look at the contents—the borrowed money off the streets of New Jersey went inside my coat, ready to finish paying for Bea's release.

"I'll be sending all I can each month. It should be around $200. I appreciate your help with the loan, more than you'll ever know."

"Well, I guess this makes me your Uncle Max," Duano said.

I nodded back.

The wide silver bow of the ferry boat came into view. It stopped in practiced fashion, and three crew members fixed the boat to the dock with thick lines.

I walked to the end of the pier and stepped onto the ferry, where passengers were met by a crewmember who smiled.

"Ticket, please." He put one punch in the paper voucher then returned it to me.

I could smell the fumes of the ferry's diesel engine. I climbed the narrow flight of stairs up to the enclosed passenger cabin and took the front-left in the cabin.

Pulling down the small, double-hung window, I called out a final good-bye to Duano.

"Take care, paisano."

* * *

As the crossing to Seattle passed smoothly under the high gray sky, the voice inside my head kept repeating, 'I'm coming, baby.' In Seattle the top floor of the terminal was the city's main bus depot. Greyhound, Trailways and Northwest coach lines each had their own ticket counter. The largest feature of the lobby was a racetrack-style electric tote board that listed arriving and departing buses by time, carrier and gate.

A public address system filled the air with, "Now arriving at Gate 30, Trailways Number 22 from Portland." I located my bus on the tote board: Greyhound No. 14, Express to Klamath Falls/San Francisco; Gate 29; departing 12:30 p.m.

Once through the lobby, departing passengers were back outside on a long covered ramp with bus gates on either side. Each gate had a large permanent number above its passage to the bus.

At the center of the covered bus ramp stood a popcorn stand where hot yellow kernels were continuously overflowing the big popping kettle. Gray pigeons walked the floors, keeping a wide eye open for dropped kernels they could grab. The birds might scatter just before being stepped on, or simply waddle a few short steps away when brushed by a passing shoe.

At 20 minutes before noon, my bus pulled in and disgorged passengers from Reno. The motor coach was then remarked for Klamath Falls/San Francisco. After thirty minutes for a cleaning and refueling break, the public address system announced we were boarding. I chose a window seat just behind the driver. After getting underway, he drew a hanging microphone down to his face.

"Good afternoon, folks. This is the bus to Klamath Falls with continuing service to Sacramento and San Francisco. We will make a one-hour dinner stop at The Dalles and we expect to have you into Klamath Falls at about noon tomorrow. There is a restroom at the back of the bus for your comfort. My name is Louie and my driving partner is Ray. Thanks for going Greyhound."

The bus ride was anything but restful for me. My mind danced from scene to scene as I imagined a reunion with Bea. I wasn't sure if she'd be in Iowa, on the bus herself, or still at Tule Lake. Having no idea of the realities of Tule Lake or Muscatine, Iowa, my mind filled in the possible scenes as I imagined what might lie ahead.

In the theater of my mind, my first sight of Bea was her running across the lawn at Hazel's in Muscatine. I clasped my hands onto my upper arms as I imagined our first kiss. When the image faded, I relaxed, resting my head on the tall seat back. Then I imagined Bea sitting across the aisle, on her own bus, moving away from Klamath Falls.

Next, I imagined Bea running across the hard-packed dirt of the Segregation Center compound when she recognized me. We were separated by a tall wire fence. My hands overlapped hers as she gripped the wire, leaning forward and gazing into my eyes. "Darling, I knew you would come for me."

Our fingers interlocked and we clutched through the wire barrier. She cried and I comforted her with soft shushing noises like I would sooth a frightened child. Then the dream ended when the bus slowed, and I was awakened by the hiss of its air brakes.

I closed my eyes, hoping to return to the dream. I was in the camp commander's office at Tule Lake. The official across the desk silently listened as I pleaded to marry my fiancée and take her out of the camp.

"I know this can be done, as my friend Alex McLaren rescued his Japanese wife from internment."

The official shook his head, "no." Next, I offered to come and live with my beloved inside the camp. I held out the ribbon that hung around my neck with the dangling bronze medallion.

"This is the highest award from the Free Polish Navy, the Order of the Torpedo Fish."

Again, a silent "no," was his response.

Leaning over the desk, I unfolded the letter signed by Captain Olson, Commander Stillman and Commander Munson.

"See, I'm a hero. It says so right here."

I begged as the camp commander leaned forward to touch the medallion and the letter, offered up like relics of the saints.

The dream was interrupted, and I didn't get to hear the commander's answer. The drone of the road overtook my mind. By the second day on the bus I could start to smell my own unwashed body. It blended into the thickening aromas of the other 39 travelers with me in the moving metal shell.

* * *

Picking a time when the road was straight and uncrowded, I leaned forward to ask the driver a question.

"The road you take into California—Highway 97?"

"That's right," replied Louie.

"I'm making a stop to visit my aunt before I head down to San Francisco. She lives on the family farm outside of Dorris, California. I can get off when we stop in Klamath Falls, unless you would be willing to let me off at Dorris?"

"I can manage that. Sure. There's not much there, though. One other thing—I don't know if other drivers will stop for you to get back on when you're done with your visit. Dorris isn't a regular stop. So it'll be the luck of the draw for you if you can flag a bus down. You okay with that?"

"Sure, I'll figure something out." I'd take my chances with getting back on the bus at Dorris. Somehow I'd manage to travel the 10 or so miles to the Tule Lake Camp from town. I'd walk if I had to.

We arrived at noon in Klamath Falls and departed as scheduled two hours later. My unscheduled stop at Dorris came after another 45 minutes. I thanked Louie for the extra stop as he pulled my bag out from under the bus. Even at the side of the road, alone in the high desert, my heart leapt in anticipation of seeing—and perhaps saving—my lost love, who may be as close as just a few miles off in the distance. Maybe Bea was already on her own bus out to freedom? Only a visit to the camp could tell me now. Anyway, I owed Giorgio a lot, at least a visit, a handshake and a face-to-face thanks.

25.   Dorris, California, March, 1944

When I stepped off the bus I was hit by the prevailing 20 mile-per-hour wind. A blasting of fine grit left a patina on my skin and clothes. Dorris had a single paved street, a post office, a store and a bar with what passed for some food options. The upstairs rooms at the bar apparently also served as the local whorehouse. One red light in an upstairs window, always on and visible from the street, was a universal sign.

There was a motel and a Standard Oil gas station that had once probably done a good business. With the war effort requiring gas rationing, and car production changed to jeeps, tanks and trucks, a motel or gas station was a tough way to make a living.

Perhaps 20 small wooden houses fanned out on unpaved lanes from either side of the main street. Occupied or deserted, it was impossible to tell unless laundry, flowers or some other clue adorned the yard.

I took a room at the motel, advising that I'd be staying one or two days. The proprietress seemed happy to have a room rented.

"Do you know anything about visiting someone at the camp? A neighbor from my home town is here." Her hands went into the pockets of her faded house-dress.

"Who do you want to see—a GI guard?" Perhaps because my answer didn't come immediately she went on. "This isn't a Jap, is it?"

"Actually, it's both. There's a girl I went to school with who's inside, and I've also got a buddy with the MP unit,"

"Why do you want to visit a Jap?" she frowned. "All the Japs out there are the worst of the bunch. Seeing a GI I can understand, but seeing a Jap...that makes no sense to me. They don't get there for just being Japs, even though that should be enough if you ask me. But here, these are the bad Japs! Disloyal

I mean. Some wouldn't sign our loyalty oath, and others are suspected spies."

She crossed her arms, her posture now rigid. Even though she was wrong about many of the Japanese, who were held in the relocation camp and not the segregation camp, I kept quiet. She didn't look like she wanted to be educated or corrected.

Fighting down rage as if it were bile, I turned away for a moment before speaking. To get what I wanted, a lie would be better than a confrontation with this woman.

"Well, my friend—the Japanese one—her brother is serving with the 442nd in Europe. You've heard of them, haven't you? They're kicking the shit out of the Germans and the Italians. They're the fellas who rescued the Lost Battalion; and the 442nd is made up of all Japanese-Americans."

She nodded, but kept a frown on her face.

"My friend's dad was a big-time farmer in California, and he volunteered to come here to take over the camp's agricultural operation. They are still Japanese, yes, but there are some good Japanese-American citizens among those folks locked up in that camp."

"That's your business, I guess. Clem over at the Standard Station might run you out there. Offer him a couple of bucks and he'll probably do it," she replied, with an unblinking stare. Her expression never softened. "There are visiting hours every day from noon until 5 p.m., except Sundays. Check in at the office next to the main gate, and they'll direct you from there."

Over her shoulder, I saw a small satin banner fringed in gold. Two stars, one blue, one gold, adorned the background. I raised my gaze to the banner.

"Those are for your sons?" For a moment, I don't think either of us knew if she would respond to the question or just order me out.

"Yes, Danny is a Marine. He's somewhere in the South Pacific. We lost Davey. He was a submariner. His boat is overdue and presumed lost." She paused, her gaze level. "He is on the Wahoo."

I understood her loss and her anger. Somehow it calmed me down and gave context to her manner. I knew of the Wahoo from the Fairbanks-Morris poster. I didn't know the Wahoo had probably been lost. To keep our morale up, mostly we only heard about the successful attacks and the successful war patrols of the subs. We were less likely to hear about our losses. Then it hit me for the first time. I might have had something to do with the death of this woman's son. I shut my eyes momentarily to help close off the thought.

"I'm sorry. I hope your boy Danny makes it."

"Why aren't you serving?" I read an accusation in her question.

"I built torpedoes for the Navy, and now I'm going to build subs, so I am serving."

"Oh..." and she paused before continuing. I think that in her mind I had tilted on the edge of worthlessness, but been saved by my contribution as a defense worker.

"Go see Clem," she said, as she turned to stare at the banner and I turned away from the counter. Thanking her as I walked out, I left to find Clem at the gas station.

Clem eyed me warily but responded to my now-perfected lies, then wiped the grease from his palms onto the existing grease stains on his coveralls. He agreed that for the small fortune of $5 he would run me out to camp and bring me back. He'd wait two hours for me. If I wanted more time, it would cost me another $5.

Arriving at the Segregation Center parking lot, Clem reminded me that I had bought two hours of time and that was all. The camp was guarded by regular Army troops since a riot in the fall of 1943. A War Relocation Authority civilian staff still administered the relocation camp but the segregation camp was under Army jurisdiction.

I went first to the main gate. The machine guns were aiming not down the road on which I'd just arrived but toward the double-wire fence. White latex condoms had been rolled down over their muzzles like so many erections, to keep the omnipresent desert dust from fouling the barrels. One of two guards came out of his office to meet me—a steel helmet on his head, a web belt around his waist, and a pistol hanging at his side.

"I'm passing through and wanted to say hello to an old friend, Giorgio Pelligrini. He's a medic at the clinic for the detainees. I'm with the Bureau of Ordnance and am changing stations from Keyport to Mare Island. Here are my orders and my ID," I said, offering the items before being asked.

The sentry looked from my orders to my picture ID and then back to me.

"Wait here and I'll see if I can locate your pal."

I nodded my thanks and stood silently looking along the fence at the guard towers. Through the double set of wire fences, row after row of squat gray buildings were set along board sidewalks that ran from the building doors to wide dirt streets. Any signs of color, other than gray, were lacking. I hoped Bea had already gone. The prospect of her being behind the wire that loomed in front of me made my stomach clench and my anal sphincter tighten.

Stepping back outside his door the guard spoke.

"Hey, McBride, Sergeant Pelligrini is on duty. He says he can take a break to say hello. He'll be over here in about five minutes. You should wait over there at the guard gate," he said, pointing to a man-door through the double fences.

"Thanks," I said with a wave, and I moved to the designated spot and waited. I was glad that I had a description of Giorgio from Duano.

Duano had also described me to Giorgio. He waved as he walked up to the inner, wire-covered door. The gate guard hailed another guard inside the wire by the man-door and the door was opened. Giorgio was allowed through the two doors, while I was motioned to stay put.

We hugged each other, exchanging back slaps.

"We're old friends," I whispered in his ear. "You're glad to see me."

"We probably met in reform school then," he whispered back. "Come on, I'll find us a cup of coffee and some privacy. Jeez, it's great to see you, Pat," he said, extra loudly so the guards could hear. "Follow me."

We walked back to the guard shack. Giorgio spoke to the same guard that I'd seen. Then he motioned for me to follow and we entered the guard station, walking through the office and into a second room. It was the guards' break room. A coffee urn, cups and condiments sat in one corner.

In another corner, a poster showed a cartooned sailor wearing a pointed dunce cap writing on a blackboard—"I should have gone to the pro-station," over and over. Under it was a small table with an open wood box filled with condoms and brown paper packets. "E. P. T.—PRO-KIT, Individual Chemical Prophylactic (For Protection from Venereal Disease.)" I picked up a packet and read the contents: "1) Tube containing 5 grams of ointment; 2) Instruction sheet; 3) Soap impregnated cloth; 4) Cleansing tissue."

Holding up the packet, I turned to Giorgio.

"What's up with this?"

"The Army loses about 600 soldiers per day to the clap. These are free condoms that the guys can take before going off post. The E.P.T. packets are here just in case you forgot to wrap your rascal. In some units it's an Article 15, that's an administrative punishment, but if you're a cook or an MP it can cost you a stripe or get you a court martial. So, if one of these guys thinks he may have dipped his pen in the wrong ink, he can use one of these. Squeezes the ointment into his pecker, massages it up inside and hopes that he beat the bugs."

I tossed the kit back into the box.

"Guys don't use the EPT's unless they're desperate, because the ointment burns. I'm told it's like pissing fire."

Couches with metal frames lined the walls, their dark green vinyl upholstery marred by cracks and burn marks. Smoke from thousands of cigarettes had fused into the walls. It blended with the smell of burned coffee from pots that had managed to boil themselves dry.

Giorgio sat down first, choosing a corner spot, and motioned for me to sit on the couch to his right. I scooted my couch closer to his, creating a small amount of privacy for our conversation. We each leaned in toward the other, even while the room was free of intruding guards.

"It's good to meet you," said Giorgio. "Anyone that can put up with Duano has to be all right. I can't get you inside the wire. It's strictly controlled-access. I don't have a car either, so I'm stuck out here. That's why I got the P.O. Box in Newell, which is just outside the gate on the other side of the camp. So, this will have to do. I'm on a break from the clinic. If anybody comes in, we're talking about our days back home. Understand?"

"Understood and thanks for your help. I've got the rest of the money here," I tapped the breast pocket of my jacket.

"How's Bea? Has she left yet?" My question prompted a raise of his hand and a long silence.

"Look, I've got bad news. I'm sorry." He leaned closer, his forearms resting on his knees as he spoke to me.

"She's still here and he, you know who we're talking about; he is gone and your five thousand is gone with him. He wasn't at his usual post when I checked two days ago. His replacement at the guard shack said that he shipped out for the Pacific. That's all I know about him."

My eyes were downcast, my hands balled into fists.

"That thieving cocksucker," I said.

"Yeah, I know," Giorgio replied. "It gets worse...I'm sorry. I saw her at sick call at my clinic back in the second week of February."

My eyes held his gaze as my jaws tightened.

"She had some injuries. A cut lip, a cut behind one ear, and the nurse told me there were bruises on her arms, shoulders and back. She said she'd fallen down, but we suspected that she'd been attacked."

My unblinking gaze didn't waiver from Giorgio's face as he continued.

"Your girl doesn't know who I am or how I'm involved. Even though this is Tule Lake, not all of us hate all of them. The nurse had a private conversation with her, woman to woman, and tried to get her to tell what had happened. Finally, she broke down crying. She told the nurse that she had been assaulted. We took the required oral, anal and vaginal swabs to culture for venereal diseases and treated her cuts."

"Who did this to her?" The words sounded mechanical to my own ears as I fought to contain my rage.

"She refused to say who attacked her. At first, we assumed it was another one of the detainees. Finally, she told the nurse that it was an MP by the name of Gladney. Gladney was the same guy that was supposed to get her out. Your girl was absolutely terrified that if she reported him he'd hurt her mother."

"What did he do to her?"

"Betty, the nurse, told me that your girl described the whole thing, every word. No emotion, just a flat monotone delivered with an unblinking gaze off into space."

"What...did...he...do...to...her!" I repeated, my knuckles turning white as I gripped the couch cushion, my anger no longer hidden.

176

"Look Pat, you don't want to know, because it will just eat your insides. I'll tell you this much more. When the cultures came back from our lab, she had a venereal infection—gonorrhea—in her throat. We called her back in and shot her up with penicillin. She'll be fine, now. Well, physically fine, anyway."

I grabbed Giorgio's upper arm and focused on his eyes.

"Tell me now...all of it."

So he did, and he was right...I didn't want to know. Every word and detail of the attack was now stamped in my brain, just as it would be forever burned in hers. I should have listened to Giorgio, had I only known that I wouldn't stop reliving her new victimization.

"He can't get away with this!" I said, glaring at Giorgio as I slammed my fist down on the arm of the couch.

Just then, two guards came into the coffee room, laughing. Their laughing stopped when they caught sight of us.

"Who is this?" one guard asked Giorgio.

"I'm just saying hello to an old pal. He's on his way from the Navy at Bremerton to Mare Island in California. Believe it or not, he wanted to see this shit hole," Giorgio answered back. "Your sergeant said we could have a visit here, since he isn't allowed behind the wire."

The two fixed themselves mugs of coffee and took seats across the room.

"Wait until we get outside, okay?" Giorgio said, his hands out flat, palms down. "Anyway, I better get back to the clinic before my boss has a shit fit." He rose and indicated I should follow him. Out of ear-shot he added the rest of what he knew.

"I reported the assault to the MP company commander, and that Gladney had the clap. The major told me that he'd look into the alleged attack and get back to my commanding officer."

"Good," I replied.

"Not so much. I was told Gladney had shipped for the South Pacific and, in view of that, they would have Gladney checked for VD when he arrived at his new post. Personally, I think his commander thought she'd probably been attacked by another detainee, and that she was looking for a free shot at the Army."

"Son-of-a-bitch," I hissed through clenched teeth.

"She's still here, but if you mention the incident, all you're going to get is tears or total silence—maybe both. If I find out anything more about the other guy, I'll pass the word to Duano."

Leaving the guard shack, I asked him to pass some details on to Duano in any case.

"Thanks for everything. I'll try to see her tomorrow. About the loan from Duano; if I can't figure out another angle, I'll send it back to him."

We shook hands, clapped backs and pledged to stay in touch, just like any two long-time friends. I walked back to Clem's truck, shaking my head and wondering how I, or anyone, could find himself so victimized and powerless...twice.

I hoped that some Jap would put a bayonet up Gladney's ass.

* * *

The next morning, Clem drove me back to Tule Lake. He leaned out the driver's window to remind me, "Just two hours now."

Inside the office, a waiting area was separated from a working area by a simple wooden counter. The walls held framed pictures of the other nine WRA camps. Also pictured was the Tule Lake facility, shot sometime before the creation of the segregation camp.

"Can I help you?" one of two clerks asked, looking up from her desk.

"I'd like to visit one of your guests."

"We have no guests here. Just Japs," came the reply, and her eyes returned to her desk.

Her slur burned in my ears, so I waited a moment before speaking.

"Look, I came a long way to see an old school friend. Can you help me or not?"

Rising from her seat this time, she took a legal-size form out of a drawer hidden under the counter.

"Fill this out." Turning, she walked back to her desk and sat down. I stared at the form.

"Pencil, please."

Removing a pencil from her top desk drawer, she stepped to the counter and slammed it down in front of me, without making eye contact. My "thank you" went unanswered.

I looked at the detailed form: Who do I want to see? What is my business with this detainee? Who am I? Where do I live and work? Completing the form, I coughed, hoping to catch her attention. It didn't.

"Okay, I'm done with the form."

Rising again, she collected my completed form. She studied the contents. Seconds turned to minutes as I waited at the counter. Finally, her expressionless face lifted from the form. I watched her check a multi-drawer card file, thumbing through the cards in the section marked with the letter 'S.'

"She is allowed visitors. If you'll take a seat, I'll call inside the camp and have her brought out—if we can locate her."

Picking up a black telephone receiver she dialed three numbers, waited and then spoke into the phone.

"We have a visitor here now for No. 82308300—Sakai, Beatrice. Her card says she's housed in Dormitory 808. Her work station is in the school, Room 12. She's a math teacher."

Answering a question from the other end of the line she answers, "Patrick E. McBride." She hung up the phone and went back to other work as I took a seat.

After a few more minutes, the phone rang.

"Reception, Mrs. McDowell speaking. I'll tell him. Thank you." Then she hung up.

"Miss Sakai is refusing the visit. Sorry."

I could tell she was lying about being sorry. Her gaze returned to her desk top.

"Thank you. I appreciate your help." I lied about appreciating her help.

"Say, do you folks have a gift shop here? I'm trying to find one of those posters...the ones that say, "Kill a Jap for Jesus," you know?"

"No gift shop here, but you might try the store in town," she said, smiling for the first time as I walked out.

Walking back outside to Clem's truck, I got in.

"They couldn't find her at the moment," I said, lying about what happened. "Can I buy another two hours tomorrow?"

"Sure, for another $5."

I arranged to meet Clem at the gas station the next day for the trip back out.

* * *

After dinner in the bar and not yet ready to surrender to the solitude of a cheap room alone, I walked out along the road toward the camp. It was a warm night; crickets chirped, and the smell of sage was all around.

"Livestock," read the sign above an arrow that pointed down the road just out of sight of the town. A mile along the dirt road a small house, all alight, came into view. Perched in a glider swing on the covered front porch was a girl. I turned and smiled as I walked past.

"Are you looking for some company darling? I'm a virgin. I'm absolutely clean." She put a cigarette to her lips. "Can you light me up? I'm out of matches," her eyes held me in a steady gaze.

Walking over to the swing, I lit her cigarette. She patted the seat with her hand without speaking. I sat, not for the proffered sex, but for something even more basic—company. She looked to be in her mid-teens, a slim peroxide blonde sitting in the fading light. A pink chenille robe, too large by half, covered her from neck to mid-ankle.

"I'm Mary."

Removing the cigarette and tapping off the ash on the arm of the swing, she moved her knee so that the robe drifted open to display her thigh. Small wisps of red hair curled out from under the seam of her robe.

"Five dollars, what do you think? You'll be glad you did," she smiled, fixing me with her eyes. No words passed back as my thumb tamped tobacco into my pipe.

"I really am a virgin, you know. I did have a riding accident once, though." Her eyes were wide as she tilted her head slightly and asked, "You believe me, don't you, mister?"

"Thanks for the offer, but I'm just walking before I head in for the night. You know, Mary, I think you can do better than this. Maybe get to Portland or Tacoma and get a job in a defense plant. They need virgins to help with the war effort, too." I smiled and lit my pipe as I got up to go.

"Don't go. I'm just lonely. If I go back inside, the old bag that runs the place will just boss me around more and make me clean the kitchen. How about $3? I'm worth it, you'll see."

Turning my back to the porch, I kicked rocks with the toe of my boot.

"Listen, take me back to town with you, and I'll do yah for free. You're right. I hate this place, and I want to be somewhere else—be somebody else." Her voice dropped. "I'm really Mildred from Madras, Oregon. Pretty dull huh? Madras is the only place

I know that is actually worse than here. The whole place smells like you need to check the bottom of your shoes. There's nothing out there but jack rabbits and cows. If I'd stayed around Madras I might have ended up the pump for some older rancher who only smacked me around when he got too drunk to get it up. So I took off just as soon as I was old enough to butcher; if you know what I mean."

I stopped kicking, and we were both silent as crickets rustled off in the fading light. Walking back to the swing I reached out and put my hand on top of her shoulder.

"You're fine just who you are, Mildred. You'll make it out of this prison. I'm sure of it, because I can see that you are better than this place...or this job." I bent and kissed her hand before walking off.

* * *

It was a 15-minute drive from town to the camp, so I picked 2:30 for our departure. This would put me there at the end of Bea's teaching day, but before she left the school, so her whereabouts would be known to the camp staff. The two clerks had changed; perhaps I got the relief help the day before. A little educated on the drill now, I asked for a Visitation Request Form and a pencil.

I filled out a new form. Handing over the completed paper, I was asked for photo identification. Again, there was a call made, and again there was a wait, so I paced the room. When the clerk's phone finally rang back, she listened and then thanked the other speaker.

"She doesn't want to see you. Sorry."

Pressing my luck, I asked if they could give Miss Sakai a message.

"Sorry, we're not allowed to pass messages to the detainees."

"Look, this is important. Miss Sakai used to care for my mom. Mom died and I wanted Bea to know. It was my mom's dying request—that I let Bea know of her passing and thank her for all her kindness," I lied. "All I want is for Bea to know that I'm going to keep coming back until she agrees to see me. I promised Mom."

"Do you want me to inform her of your mother's passing? I guess I could do that."

"Thanks so much," I lied. "That's a kind offer, but she and Mom were close. I don't want Bea to get the bad news from a stranger. You can understand," I said, my head lowered slightly to look more sympathetic.

"Look, I'll do what I can to get her here, and I won't mention that your mother has passed. Come back tomorrow at the same time."

Back with Clem, I renewed our deal as we drove back to the motel. The faded paint on the cinderblock walls of my room seemed to fit with the dull colors of town and desert outside my one window. Thankfully what passed as a diner, doubled as a bar. At least the beer was cold,

* * *

Three bad meals later, I was back before the same clerk. She smiled sympathetically.

"Sorry about your mom. The detainee will be here in about ten minutes."

"Do I need to fill out a new Visitation Request Form?"

She shook her head and pointed to a door on my right.

"Through there to the visitation area. You can have 30 minutes to visit. All our visits are supervised, but the guard is not interested in what you say so much as that you don't pass anything to the detainee—just so you know."

Through the door was the visitor's room—gray walls, a counter and four sets of wooden chairs bolted to the floor, each chair facing the other on opposite sides of the counter. Wooden partitions separated each set of chairs into small lengths of counter space. Clear plastic shields, a grid of holes drilled to allow sound to pass, blocked all touch between visitor and detainee. A large clock hung on the wall at the end of the row of partitioned spaces. I marked off the 30 minutes in my mind. A guard sat above my right shoulder on a platform in the center of the wall. He looked down on the detainees from his high post inside an open loft. I chose to sit at the first set of chairs, just inside the door. I'd never been in a prison or a jail before, but I was clearly in a prison now. My beloved was in prison. This place was worse than I had ever imagined. Tule Lake existed to punish people...for the crime of being Japanese.

A door behind the counter opened at the opposite end of the room. Bea entered. The woman I had known was not there before me—something was missing. It was more than just her faded dress or dull hair. There seemed to be no one home behind her hollow, vacant eyes. The healing of her lip and the cut corner of her mouth showed as two dark lines that had scabbed over. It scared me, and I was ashamed for what had happened to this once-joyful girl. I stood up and, recognizing me, she pivoted on her heels to leave.

Rushing to the farthest interview space, I put my face to the plastic.

"Please! Please, just stay and hear me out for a little while."

Turning back to the chair and counter, she sat down. Her gaze was low enough to avoid my eyes.

"You shouldn't have come. They lied to me. I wouldn't be here if I had known it was you. Please go." She rose, as if to leave.

"I can't go—not until we talk. I'll just keep coming back, because you have never been out of my life...only out of my sight. Please just sit with me for a little while and hear me out."

She sat back down.

Controlling my breathing, I hoped to slow the pounding of my heart. Bea's gaze didn't rise from the hands in her lap. It was not only the plastic shield that was keeping us apart. Invisible, but just as real, was the barrier of what Bea had lived through during the past months.

"I never hurt you, and I've loved you since grade school. I'm sorry for what happened to your family and the store. I couldn't stop any of it, but they were all wrong—the government, the people in San Bruno that burned the store and shunned your family, and that asshole Mr. Craig. They were all wrong.

"But Bea, I'm not them. It's me, the boy with the hoe working in your dad's field. I'm the one fishing next to you, and holding your hand at the show. It's just me and I want you back. We can get through this...we can be us again."

Leaning forward, with my forearms on the counter, I whispered.

"I'm still here. I've tried to find a way to get you out of here. I got together all my money. I borrowed even more and bribed a crooked guard to smuggle you out. Margie helped me find a safe place for you to go. Duano helped me keep track of how you were. I just found out that the guard took my money and left you here.

"I had it all arranged. You had a new identity, a place to stay in Iowa, money for you and a wedding ring from me. He robbed us both and I'm so sorry. But I'll find another way...or another guard."

"No, not again," she whispered back.

"What happened to your face?" I asked.

Bea raised her face to mine, and I saw a questioning look. She opened her mouth to speak but no words came out. She may have wondered if I knew what had happened, but she neither asked me if I knew nor hinted that I did.

"Are you all right?" I asked.

She spoke slowly, her eyes focused on the counter that still concealed her hands.

"The guard said that he'd been paid to get me out. He showed me the money that he'd found in the book, and the ring. He showed me the letter and said it was for me, then put it in his pocket. He said, 'I've got other plans for you. This letter is my insurance, so that you, your boyfriend nor anyone else will ever tell the Army about what I'm going to do.' Then he ..."

Lowering my voice even more I said, "Bea, I'm so sorry. I did everything I could think of to get you out of this hell-hole. I had it all worked out so that by the time you were missed, you'd be safe in Iowa with Margie's relatives and a new name. God, I'm so sorry."

"I know what you tried to do for me. It was a kind and loving thing to do, and I'll never forget it."

Tears began to overflow her eyelids. Her silence became unbearable for me. As gently as I could, I asked again. Her hands went to the counter and she began to push herself to her feet.

"He got away with it because I'm Japanese, and to him that makes me less than human." I heard anger in her voice for the first time.

"He's the same as the man who shot Dad. We're just Japs, not really people. Your country doesn't see me like you do and it never will." She started to rise from the chair.

"Please, don't go, Bea."

Her tears fell onto the counter behind the plastic. Finally her shoulders relaxed and fell as she seemed to give up her urge to flee. I let the silence remain until she lifted her head.

"When you wrote your good-bye letter to me, you said that you hadn't stopped loving me. You said that the country was afraid of you because of your family name. When we're back together, your name will be the same as mine, so no one will be afraid. They were wrong in what they did to you, to your family...and to us."

Bea's open palm went to the glass, and I placed my own hand over hers on the opposite side. "Oh, Pat," was all she managed to say.

"You told me in that letter that you never doubted my love. To show you how much I love you, I did something. I love you more than I love my country, my family or my life."

"Pat, what did you do?"

"I've made the government pay—pay big. I've hurt them, truly I have. When we are finally alone, I'll tell you how they paid. I hit them where they feel it most, in the wallet! I know there is nothing that can undo what your family has suffered— what you have suffered—but I've tried to balance the scales. I've done all I could do because you matter that much to me.

"Please, I can see how sad you are and how empty you must feel inside. Please, Bea. I'm not one of them. I never hurt you and I never will. We can get married, and I'll take you away from this terrible place. Just like Margie and Alex. You'll be safe and free."

Something came into her eyes as she raised her gaze to my face. Her eyes looked brighter now, but the brightness was tears.

"Oh, Pat, it's too late. I don't want you to hurt anybody. It's been twenty-two months since Dad was killed. It's not just the time that has passed. You may be the same sweet boy that I fell in love with, but I'm not the same naïve girl that I was.

"What happened to our safe childhood place? How could San Bruno people have turned on us? They burned the store. My *mother* is locked up in this prison."

Her voice faltered, as she fought back tears.

"She's feared by one country and afraid to return to the other. The meanness of the guards and staff everywhere—all these things each wounded me even more. Finally, my wounds have started to heal. Some are still ugly scabs, while others have turned to scars, but at least I'm starting to heal. I can't face or risk hurting anymore. I'm just not strong enough. I grew up thinking that I was an American because this is where I lived...but my mother was right."

There was only silence between us again. I stared at her as my throat began to constrict, and my eyes felt the first dampness of tears trying to overflow. I started to panic.

"What does that mean?"

"You see me as American. But the rest of them, they see me as Japanese. I understand now that wherever I am, wherever I live, I'll always be Japanese. The choice was never really mine...or ours."

"Tell me what to do, and I'll do it. I'll do anything for you—for us. I'll beg if you want me to."

"No please, please don't."

Bea's body seemed to shake as if inescapable chills had overtaken her. As I watched and heard her voice, I prayed she wouldn't collapse before my eyes, just out of reach. I didn't know what to do. I had nothing left to say.

We sat in silence until she spoke again.

"There's someone else now. His name is Tom. He is Japanese and he's broken too, like me, but together we make almost one whole person. I would have killed myself if I hadn't found him. Writing my last letter to you was the hardest thing I've ever had to do. I thought I would die—and I did die inside for so long.

"Please, leave me behind. Don't hurt anybody for me. You'll only hurt yourself. Being with you outside might be wonderful, now. But truly, I believe it would be terrible. The country out there, beyond the wire, doesn't want me, even if you do. Inside the wire, even in this terrible place, this is our place, our ghetto, and I can live here. I can't face your world outside the wire. I can't leave Mom or Tom. I'm just too scared."

My own tears welled up, about to fall.

"If only you knew how much I've done for us, you'd know just how much I love you, and how much I made everyone that hurt you pay. Please, Bea."

My hand stayed pressed to the plastic divider and tears began to run down my cheeks. Bea put her hands in her lap. This moment together was not the reunion I dreamt about; instead it was our good-bye. I wiped my eyes and tried to smile. Her tears continued to fall, and she shook her head, looking back into my face.

Getting up, she spoke quietly.

"Please go, Pat. Good-bye."

She rose, turned and walked out, head down. I knew she was lost to me even before the door closed. The clock on the wall showed that my life had changed forever in just 19 minutes.

* * *

I stayed seated long enough to dry my eyes and get control of my voice. Leaving the visitation room, passing back through the office, I kept my eyes pointed towards the floor. The sunlight stabbed them when I emerged, but not as much as the hurt that racked my insides. My head buzzed because the faint hope my sabotage had given me had slipped away. Closing my eyes for a moment, I said to myself, "Relax, relax, relax," over and over.

The image of Donald Robbins, slouching drunk in Einar's chair, flashed before my mind's eye. I heard his voice again.

"I'm dead; I'm so dead."

The specter of Robbins no longer slouched or head-down, filled my mental view.

"Welcome aboard, Pat. Please join me. Being dead is no fun, but the worst part is being alone as I walk among the living. We'll do it together. You tell me about Bea, and I'll tell you about Colin. It'll pass the time. You'll see."

As I came back to the here and now of Tule Lake, the image of Robbins faded from my mind. His face was gone, but his words lingered. "I'm dead."

I looked myself over, like an accident victim, checking for visible wounds. Whatever had been torn or broken remained invisible, but I could feel my injury, even if I couldn't see it.

After a few minutes with the warmth of the sun on my face, the panic attack playing out inside my head faded. It had never occurred to me that Bea would not be moved by what I had done, by the price I had exacted from the government. Hoewever, standing in the parking lot with Clem honking his horn, I knew she was lost to me. There simply was no us anymore.

Finally, the inside of my head was still. The stillness was as cold and quiet as the bottom of a well.

I recalled the day Mr. Sakai had advised me what to do in the face of a seemingly insurmountable, catastrophic disaster.

"Pat, you pick up your hoe and just keep working. You don't have to work fast, just keep looking ahead and focus on your work."

* * *

Out in the parking lot, I got back in Clem's truck.

"Clem, can I get you to drive me in to Klamath Falls? I've got a bus to catch at 6 p.m. If you could do that for me, I'd really appreciate it. There's an extra $20, if you can make that happen. I'll need to make two quick stops, the motel and the cathouse we passed on the way here."

Clem made it happen. Pulling over in front of the little house, neither of us spoke. I got out and walked onto the porch and opened the screen door. I knocked on the wooden door and a middle-aged woman in a flowered dress appeared. Her perfume was so strong it assaulted my nose and brought tears to my eyes.

"Welcome stranger, come on in and have a look at the new livestock." She gestured to a parlor inside to the right.

"I borrowed a lighter from one of your girls, last night: Mary. I wanted to return it; if she's not busy at the moment. I'll wait on the porch."

"I'll give it to her, darling," offered the madam.

"I'd really like to thank her myself." Then seeing that courtesy was not moving the madam I added, "And see about arranging something with her for later tonight."

I took a step back as the madam smiled at the prospect of future business and turned away. On the porch I checked my wallet and took out all my cash except for the money I borrowed from Duano and $40: $20 for Clem and $20 for me to use getting home.

"Well, look who came back. Saw something you liked last night after all." Mildred from Madras, the Virgin Mary of Dorris, was still wearing her same pink robe.

"Just listen for a minute," I said in a soft voice. "I don't want the madam to hear."

Then I put my full hand into the pocket of the robe and withdrew it empty before speaking. Her eyes moved from mine and down to the pocket of her robe. Her hand went into the pocket.

"You're fine, just who you are. Today I planned to save a girl from her prison, and that girl turned out to be you," I said, as we shared a gaze.

"We all make choices and do what we think we have to do at the time. Sometimes we just get it wrong. I know. I hope you get it right next time."

I kissed her hand then turned back to Clem and his truck. I heard the screen door slam behind me. I got in Clem's truck, but when he started to pull away Mildred burst back through the door, barefooted, a pair of blue jeans on under her robe.

"Take me with you, mister, please," Mildred shouted. She clutched a flour sack that was probably stuffed with her few possessions; a faded blouse dangled from its mouth.

"Darling girl, I can't take you. I'm headed to California to work at a shipyard. "

"We'd best go," I said to Clem, trying not to look back at the panic on Mildred's face. We pulled away, leaving the slim blonde standing alone on the gravel road.

"God damn it, will you look at that," Clem bellowed, looking up into his rear view mirror.

"She's chasing the truck."

I turned just enough to see the skinny kid, robe flapping as she ran on through the cloud of dust the truck kicked up in her face. On she came as the house faded in the distance. Then, as I watched, free for a moment from painfully recalling Bea, she fell.

"Clem, pull over."

Clem pulled to the right shoulder. I watched as the Virgin of Dorris got up to her knees and began to limp on toward the truck. Her jeans were torn and blood began to fill the abrasions on her knee. Jogging back I grabbed her by the shoulders. Her face was painted with gray stripes by tears cutting channels through the dust that covered her. Her dirty feet were colored by blood that caked on the tips of several toes. The robe hung open, its seams falling straight down across budding cleavage as her chest rose and fell. I heard, then saw, Clem reversing the truck to our spot.

"I can't go back. The madam won't take me back now anyway. I can ride into town with you and be a whore in Dorris. I can walk to Newell and be a whore over there, or go back to Madras and be a whore in my home town." Her fingers were curled into tight fists.

"But, it's just...I'd rather kill myself than be a whore anymore."

From the silence that followed, I believed her. More silence followed as I took the sack from her hand and pulled out the faded blouse.

"Get dressed," I said, and I turned her back to me, not wanting to see her nakedness. She turned around as she buttoned the final button. Putting my arm around her waist, I walked her to the cab of the truck. She sat between us and I nodded for Clem to drive back to town and my motel.

"Go have some coffee, I'll be ready to go in half an hour," I told Clem.

"Go up to my room and clean yourself up as best you can. I'll be along in a minute," I said, and passed her the room key.

Walking toward the store, I had no plan for Mildred beyond the knowledge that I could neither leave her in her prison, nor abandon her. I believed her when she said she'd kill herself. In the store I bought gauze, peroxide, cotton socks, canvas shoes and a small man's windbreaker.

When I returned to my room, the door was unlocked. At the bathroom sink she'd cleaned her face with a wet cloth and washed the dust out of her short peroxide blonde hair, which now hung like a white shower cap over her scalp.

"Sit here," I said, pointing to the toilet, lid down.

She sat.

Taking the peroxide and gauze from the paper bag, I cleaned her knee and toes with the wash cloth and then the peroxide. She made not a sound and never took her eyes off me when I kneeled at her feet trying to encase her toes in protective gauze.

"Why?" was all she asked.

I shook my head; there was no answer that could be shared.

"See if you can put these on." I held up the white socks and canvas shoes.

"I need to write a note. When you're ready we've got to go. I've got—we've got—busses to catch."

In the single drawer of the small desk was a pencil, three sheets of letter-size paper and two envelopes.

Dear Mrs. Olson,

I need a big favor. This is my friend Mildred from Madras, Oregon. She needs a job and a safe place to stay. I'd appreciate anything that you or Florence could do for her. She's a good person who just needs a little help.

Thanks for everything.

Pat McBride

On the outside of the envelope I wrote instructions for Mildred.

At the Seattle train station, go downstairs and take the Black Ball ferry to Keyport, WA. See Mrs. Lena Olson at the mercantile. Give Mrs. Olson this letter. If the store is closed, go to the café and ask for Florence.

She touched my shoulder as I sealed the letter.

"I'm ready to go. Are you?" to which she nodded.

Leaving the room key on the desk I passed her the denim windbreaker and we walked outside. Clem was already in his truck. Mildred clutched her sack of worldly goods, and I put my suitcase in the truck bed. We rode in silence to Klamath Falls. Arriving outside the Greyhound depot, I passed Clem a folded $20 bill.

"I'm sorry about the camp" he said, then paused, "and good luck with this one."

"I thought that I hid my feelings better than that. Guess not."

Clem drove off.

Suitcase in hand, we walked into the store that displayed the Greyhound Bus logo in its window. At the counter, I bought a one-way ticket to Seattle and asked the departure times for Mildred's bus. Thirty minutes for her to wait and another hour for me after that. We sat down to wait outside on the worn wooden bus bench.

"Here's the deal," I said, handing over her ticket and the letter I'd prepared. She took them both, studying each before starting to speak.

"Don't," I squeezed her hand to stop her. "This is all I can do for you, to give you a new start. You're not a whore anymore. You get to be a virgin again. Remember the riding accident." We waited, holding hands in silence, until her bus pulled in.

"Find a nice guy who'll treat you like a lady. Don't settle for anything less. Now, get on the bus."

She climbed the two steps, showed her ticket to the driver and walked down the aisle and out of view. For a moment she was in a window seat staring back at me. Then she was gone.

26.   San Bruno, March, 1944

Riding the bus for another day back to the Bay Area would have been a great time to think about my past and my future, but I didn't. To lessen my pain, I forced myself to banish any thoughts of Bea that came into my mind. In Sacramento, I used a pay phone to let Dad know my arrival time. My plan for revenge at Keyport had been a success, but it had done me no good.

Dad and Mom met me at the bus stop in San Bruno. Dad shook my hand and Mom hugged me.

"You look tired," was Mom's first comment.

"It was a long trip, Mom. It feels good to not be moving."

I didn't tell my folks anything about what I had learned out in the high desert at Tule Lake. Putting my case in the trunk of their Buick, I paused.

"I've been sitting for a long time. I'd like to walk a bit and have a look at the town. I'll see you guys at home for dinner." My dad shrugged and Mom's smile momentarily dimmed as they got back into the Buick and drove home.

Standing alone at the bus stop at Jenevein and El Camino, I was ten steps from the vacant lot where the Sakai's garden shop had been. The lot had been scraped bare of debris, but the ash from the fire was still visible between the weeds that now grew where camellias and rhododendrons had thrived. Walking into the lot I found the cement slab that had once been the garden shop floor—the only remaining footprint of the Sakai family business. The coolness of the lath house and the earthy smell of the garden shop were gone.

I began walking north through the downtown and towards Tanforan. The grandstand was still there and I saw the parking lot, track, infield and stables. The stables were still configured for human occupants and not horses. Beyond the stables, what had once been open pasture on one edge of the property had become government housing.

"Welcome to Linden Village!" read a banner that hung above a new street that intersected the El Camino before heading off into rows and rows of small identical houses. They were truly ugly, yet beautiful when compared to the assembly center where Bea, her mother and brother had been housed in a converted stable.

I continued walking, crossing four lanes of traffic. I bypassed the guarded Twelfth Naval District gate and turned at the far edge of the property onto Sneath Lane. Across from the barbed wire fence of the naval property was the ornamental iron fence of the Golden Gate National Cemetery that now occupied the once-bare ground. The poppies were gone, replaced by graves. I walked below the tall eucalyptus trees. After a while, the green cemetery lawn with its rows of simple white headstones abruptly stopped. The ground changed from new grass to bare soil waiting to be filled. The graves, the grass and the bare dirt were simultaneously beautiful and awful. I turned away to look instead at the giant trunks that enfolded me under their blue-green canopy. The strong camphor scent of the trees mixed with the smells of bare earth and grass.

I headed home to my parents, having seen enough.

27.   Vallejo, March, 1944

On Monday morning, March 13, 1944, I reported to Mare Island. Before the war, Mare Island had been our Navy's only West Coast shipyard. Its wartime expansion had erased all signs of the original marshy confluence where the Napa River flowed into an arm of San Francisco Bay. The yard was now one of six West Coast facilities that built or repaired Navy vessels.

My dad insisted on driving me to the new job, despite my protests about the trip using up most of his gas ration stamps. I left him at the gate and walked with my bag to the guard shack. Showing my packet from Keyport, I was allowed in and spent my first day arranging pay, photo ID badge and housing.

By mid-afternoon, I was ready to be picked up by a Bureau of Ships official and taken to my work station—a three-room building at the end of a dock. I would be working on the new subs that were tied up alongside.

My new boss from the Bureau of Ships used one room for his office. Our lockers, shower-room and day-room filled another. The third room was a large tool crib that held all the equipment needed to install and tune the four powerful OP diesel engines for each boat.

My first sub was the *USS Lionfish*. My job was the installation of her four diesels, their synchronizing and the unique challenges of perfecting diesel engines for silent and vibration-free operation. She was commissioned in August 1944 and sailed for the South Pacific.

Even after the formal Japanese surrender in September 1945, I continued working on the submarines that were under construction at the end of the war.

Mare Island put 25 of the new Balao subs in the water before the war ended. Four hulls were in progress at any one time, with each one getting its 10-cylinder, OP diesel engines installed by my crew. We made them go, while the new Mark 18 electric torpedoes from Keyport made them fierce.

In January 1946, I helped decommission the *Lionfish*. Working around its skeleton crew, we talked frequently about her war patrols. I learned that after the start of 1944, the Navy had figured out Newport's mistakes, the faulty firing pins and the inaccurate depth setting gauges that had plagued the Mark 14s.

As 1944 progressed, most of our subs preferred to carry both the old Mark 14 and the new Mark 18 electrics that were now available. The Navy liked the electric torpedoes because they left no trail of bubbles. By 1946, the last of the Mark 14s were gone.

I had coffee on board the *Lionfish* with the men who comprised the small crew that stayed with her until she was decommissioned. It was then that I got the first real information about the effects of what I had done back at Keyport.

"We liked the Mark 14s for night attacks, because they were so much faster. The only thing the Navy never solved was that sometimes a Mark 14 would just go dead in the water—they just seemed to quit. That scared the shit out of us, especially if we were shooting at a Jap destroyer."

I've thought about that submariner's comment, "Sometimes they just seemed to quit." I had cost them money, maybe millions. It didn't make me feel bad when I first heard it, but now, every time I replay the phrase in my mind, it brings me to a door in my mind I've tried to keep closed and locked. Had I caused anyone to be killed as I extracted my monetary revenge?

28.   San Francisco, March, 1946

Andy, Duano and I stayed in touch. Andy bought a home near the Army Ammunition Plant at McAlister, Oklahoma. He liked the town and wrote that Oklahoma possum was even better than its Arkansas cousin. Duano stayed at Keyport until the war ended. In February 1946, he moved to a new job at the Naval Undersea Test Station in Bayview, Idaho, located on the southern tip of Lake Pend Oreille. He said that the sky, the mountains and the lake were all clean, and that he wanted to bathe in the cleanness of the place.

March 1, 1946, was my first day back at the San Francisco rail yard—more than five and a half years after my departure. Dallas Long had passed away. No longer only a machinist, I was the shift foreman in the diesel locomotive shop. On the shop floor, I stopped at my old bench; still a grinder's station, just not mine anymore. Wiping my index finger across the bench top, I looked at its track left in the fine metal dust. The smudge on my fingertip made me wonder—would they notice? No, probably not. Only a grinder would notice what I recognized.

Back in San Francisco, I happened to meet a girl I had never noticed during high school. Pamela Brown and I met for the first time since school in the railroad yard business office where she had come to work during the war. We married in less than four months. Pam, with her amber hair and buxom figure, was the polar opposite of Bea.

Duano made good on a promise to visit me, meet Pam and see the sights. Pam and I picked him up at the Ferry Building in San Francisco. I had returned the $1,000 I'd borrowed from him, and the unused money I had taken to Tule Lake in my failed attempt to smuggle Bea out. He had part of two days to spend with us before heading on home to New Jersey. On his first night with us, we went out to dinner in North Beach, an Italian neighborhood of San Francisco.

"You guys are great. Pat, you did better than you deserve, hooking this lady. Next time we get together, you'll meet my girl, Mildred." Removing a picture from his wallet, he passed it to Pam.

"She's beautiful. Where did you meet?"

"Thanks, I sure think so too. We met in Keyport when she got hired on at our landlady's store. Can you imagine that?" beamed Duano as he passed the snapshot to me. A slim, pretty redhead in a white bathing suit smiled up at the camera from a seat on the Keyport ferry dock.

"You're a lucky man," was all I said. The Virgin of Dorris had made it out and found a guy who'd treat her like a lady. I couldn't be happier for the both of them. Mildred secret was one that I'd gladly keep.

"How about you come to work with me tomorrow?" I asked. "I'll show you the rail yard. We'll have lunch and I'll take off early, then play tour guide and show you the city. I'll take you down to San Bruno and introduce you to my folks."

"That sounds good to me." We finished our dinner with a shot of grappa.

The next morning we arrived at the Southern Pacific yard just after 7 a.m. While I was showing him around to all my crew in the machine shop, Duano commented on the noise.

"It's louder than the Fourth of July in here."

Feigning deafness, I replied, "What?" as if I couldn't hear him.

At lunch we talked about our past together.

"Whatever happened to Bea after the war?"

"I don't know. She probably married a Japanese fella named Tom. He was also interned at Tule Lake. Between what happened to her folks and what happened to her, she couldn't see us being together. Nothing I said could get her back. That's a scab that I don't voluntarily pick at."

201

"You might want to see this. Giorgio sent it to me and I saved it to pass along to you," Duano said as he passed me a folded piece of newsprint.

I unfolded the paper and was looking at a one-inch filler note in the Tule Lake camp paper from July 10, 1945.

Sergeant Craig Gladney, age 32, was found dead under suspicious circumstances according to the Washoe County, Nevada, Sheriff's office, July 1. His body was discovered by a motorist along the side of State Highway 271 in the vicinity of the Appaloosa Ranch brothel. Proprietor Joseph Giordano advised investigators that the deceased had been a patron earlier in the evening. Sergeant Gladney was on leave at the time of his death and had previously served with the 651st Military Police Detachment at Tule Lake.

"That was him," was all Duano needed to say. "I thought you'd like to know that someone took care of that asshole."

"I didn't know that you knew about the attack."

"Giorgio told me."

"Any idea who did the world this favor?"

"I can't imagine, and neither could my Uncle Joe, who owns the Appaloosa. If I had to guess, I'd say that either the Sergeant didn't know whose money he had stolen, or maybe someone thought the guy was immoral—being around a whorehouse and all—and needed to be punished for his sins. You just never know."

"Thanks," was my only reply.

I paid our tab and we left to drive around town, with me narrating as we went.

"This is the Kezar Club where Dad got arrested. We need to stop for a drink."

And we did.

Later we drove past Seal Stadium before ending up at the Character Club bar on Market Street.

"So, you think you'll stay with the job in Idaho?" I asked.

"I think I might. The Navy is closing down Camp Farragut at Bayview, but our research station is not going away. I wrote home about how pretty everything is up there. Life's good. I moved Mildred over from Keyport, and we have a little house across the bay from my work. She says that she doesn't like 'living in sin.' I plan to marry her this fall."

"If she'll still have you, paisano."

"Yeah, that's right, if she'll have me."

Clicking his glass with mine, I said, "I'll drink to that," and we did.

Pam and I put Duano on his train for New Jersey the next morning. I heard from him via letters regularly for the next couple of years. Duano and Mildred did marry in the fall. We were invited, but pleading the demands of work, I chose not to re-enter Mildred's life. I didn't want her thanks, and she didn't need to be reminded of her past. I was glad I had managed to save at least one girl from her prison by stopping at Tule Lake.

Over time, the regular letters decreased to annual Christmas cards. Receiving Duano's cards was always bittersweet, as my mind invariably went back to my long-lost love.

Prisoners of War

29.   San Francisco, 1960 – 1980

My father passed away in 1960. When Mom asked me what I wanted from among Dad's things, I didn't ask for his watch. I wanted the silver box and the Victory Medal that it contained. When she handed me the box, I asked if she knew the identity of the young girl whose picture was stamped into the center of the lid.

"Dad said that he met Johnny McCrae at Camp Souis, outside of Marseilles. The box was a gift from Princess Mary, the daughter of King George. She'd organized a movement to send a Christmas present to every soldier, sailor or nurse in uniform throughout the British Empire. British royalty took up the cause. School children shared their pennies and churches took up collections. A silver box for officers, brass for everyone else, was delivered on Christmas morning 1914. There was candy and tobacco inside each box. Anyway, the lid has the profile of the princess and her initials."

My mother stayed in her own home alone for 15 more years. After several accidental kitchen fires, a change had to be made and she came to live with us for her final three years. We had bought our house in 1965, high up on Dolores Street in the Mission District. The house had a view of Dolores Park, and I tinkered with restoring the three-story Victorian. I renovated part of our house into a little apartment for Mom. Next to her favorite over-stuffed chair on a small, triangular bookshelf sat the Japanese vase that Mom had saved from the ashes of the Sakai's garden shop.

In the fall of 1964, I saw on the evening news that Tanforan, now a racetrack again, was on fire. The blaze had started in the old, wooden grandstand, and the building was fully engulfed in flames. I drove the 10 miles down the peninsula to San Bruno. Getting as close to the grounds as the policemen and firefighters would allow, I watched the grandstand's metal roof collapse into the burning wood below. The roof's collapse produced a great expanding cloud of sparks that momentarily illuminated the sky like the white light of magnesium sky rockets on the Fourth of July. I stood and watched the fire, one person in a crowd of many.

"It's good to see this place reduced to burning rubble," I said, but no one paid any attention to my comment.

A week later, driving alone on a Sunday, I pulled off the El Camino into the old racetrack parking area and stopped the car parallel to the highway at the edge of the still-smoking black ashes. Sitting behind the wheel, as the new doo-wop version of "Blue Moon" played over the radio, I could see across the unburned oval track to the squat line of stables where the Sakais were housed in 1942. I got out and walked around the car, putting the street lights of the El Camino behind the car and me in shadow. I opened the passenger side door for more privacy, took a step back, unzipped my fly, and pissed onto the edge of the black ashes that spread out at my feet.

* * *

I read in the paper that a new biography of FDR included revelations about the president.

In October 1941, with the war in the Pacific looming, the FBI and Naval Intelligence undertook a joint investigation of "the Japanese question on the coast." This investigation was made at the specific request of President Franklin D. Roosevelt. He wanted to know if, "in the event of war with Japan, would our Japanese-American citizens be a security threat?"

The report to the president was very simple in its conclusion: "We do not want to throw a lot of American citizens into concentration camps." The investigation concluded, the answer to the president's question was, "of course not, and it was the unanimous verdict of our investigators that in case of war, they will be quiet, very quiet."

The report was ignored by Roosevelt, and more than 120,000 Japanese-Americans, many being citizens by birth, were interned. History validated the report as there was not one single incident of espionage or sabotage committed by a Japanese-American during the war. So, this is a story about the capacity of good men to do bad things. Worse yet, sometimes our solutions turn out to actually be the problem.

Reading the excerpt from the biography didn't breathe life back into the hate I had nurtured for so long. I just wanted to find some understanding of how these things came to be.

Mom passed away in her sleep in the spring 1978. My bride, Pam, passed away in the fall of 1979. An aggressive cancer, late to be discovered, had invaded her body and took her four months after the diagnosis. I'm thankful she died knowing that I truly loved her. Both of them died without being burdened by any of my secrets. I retired from the railroad in 1980, at the age of 60.

The Japanese vase that Mom had rescued from the ashes of the garden shop passed to me after her death and now sat on a shelf in my kitchen. I looked at it daily but had never studied the detail or even handled it, beyond moving it occasionally. The touch of the vase burned me with a million memories of my long-lost love and the imagined joys that never were allowed to occur. I remembered how back in 1930, Mrs. Sakai, noticing my mother's interest, walked over and stood by her side. Mrs. Sakai's words from so long ago came back to me, with Mom squeezing my shoulder in mild disapproval of me inserting my small voice into the adult conversation.

"The vase depicts a famous Japanese shrine where ancient warriors sacrificed themselves in the service of their honor, staying loyal to their master even to their deaths."

"Patrick, they were both good and bad at the same time. They were fighting their feudal governor, who was like their government, so in this way they were bad. But the governor was evil. They were fighting for somethings more important—their honor and duty to their lord. When you are older, you will maybe understand how loyalty and honor sometimes must struggle with our duty and obligations. This is how people can be both good and bad."

Taking the vase down from the top of the cabinet for dusting, I studied it for what seemed to be the first time. Looking inside, I saw an open space, meant for water and flower stems, behind the oval of the finely worked clay sculpture. Because of the Sakai's connection to flowers, it was natural that the vase would be meant for flowers, besides having its own intrinsic beauty.

I inverted the vase, and visible under the dark glaze on the bottom were two Japanese letters that probably served as the artist's signature. Falling at my feet from deep inside the overturned vase was a small roll of yellowed fabric like a scroll, tied neatly with a fine black cord. Written on the silky surface in faded black ink were four columns of Kanji characters. The silk, bleached with age, now showed as a soft white shading to ivory tones. I placed the scroll and vase on my dining room table to await further inspection.

Now curious about the provenance of the vase and its contents, I contacted our family friend Priscilla, who had written about Asian history, and asked her to look at the vase. Priscilla had been a neighbor of my parents and also knew the Sakai family. Now in her late 70s, small, tanned and wrinkled, she stood over the table regarding vase and scroll. She inspected the vase from all sides as she turned it in her hands. Seeing the letters on its underside, she confirmed what I had suspected.

"These are the artist's initials."

207

Turning the vase to its front, her right hand cradling it and her left hand holding its base firmly, she might have been looking at a precious grandchild for the first time.

"The scene in the grotto is a famous one. This is the Senjuki-ji shrine in Kyoto, Japan. It's a small temple and burial ground where a famous man and his vassals are buried. Pat, have you ever heard the story of the forty-seven Ronin?"

"When I was little, the lady that had the vase, before Mom told us a story about Ronin."

"Yes, forty-seven of the Ronin plotted for two years and finally killed the governor who destroyed their master. At their master's grave, the Senjuki-ji shrine, they committed ritual suicide. Their honor was thus restored as was the family honor of their master. Let me see if I can read the scroll you found inside the vase," Priscilla said quietly.

I waited silently while Priscilla read, mouthing the words as she translated the characters on the silk.

To my wife Taeko,

Forgive me for any pains that my actions brought upon our family. I felt like a father of two beloved children whom I prayed would get along but could not do so. It is not that I loved one above the other. I pray that you may understand that in the end, my duty to Japan was greater than my loyalty to our adopted country. Our honor is clean, my love, and we will be together again in another life.

Sakai Oishi

Her reading done, she asked me, "Interesting...do you have any idea what the writer of the scroll means, Pat?"

"I really don't know," I lied.

The fact was I knew instantly what the scroll meant. It meant Mr. Sakai had been a spy! I thanked Priscilla for her help and for

208

having been such a good neighbor for my parents. Then I showed her out.

Alone now, except for the ghosts and memories that had been thrust into my conscious mind, I took the scroll along with my pipe out to the back porch. Looking over the rooftops, I could see in the distance the cranes at the Hunter's Point shipyard on the Bay. When I lit my pipe, the breeze from the shoreline blew smoke past my head so it trailed rather than rose before me. My back to the wind, I sheltered my bronze-cased Zippo lighter until it produced a flame. The silk scroll came out from my pocket. I allowed it to unroll, then set fire to the bottom corner. Clicking the lighter shut with my other hand, I watched the flame move up the scroll. The ivory-colored material passed through shades of yellow to brown, then to black as the characters vanished before my eyes. The ashes danced briefly in the wind as they swirled away from me out over my yard and the larger city.

Epilogue

Driving down the El Camino Real in the fall of 1981, I passed the new Tanforan Mall that had replaced the racetrack. The former beauty of the flowers in the racetrack infield was gone forever, as were all signs of the track's fiery end. I turned west and skirted the neat rows of graves inside the Golden Gate National Cemetery fence.

My drive continued to Skyline Boulevard, swallowed in fog, and then down the windy road to Highway 1 and the ocean. At Linda Mar, I turned up the valley away from the beach to what had once been Sakai's field. Gone were the flowers, and in their place was a subdivision of slab-floored ranch houses. I couldn't hear the creek behind the field, or the wind rustling the leaves of the trees that shaded its banks where two innocent children first kissed. Now the creek flowed through a cement pipe buried deep underground.

Back on the coast highway, I crossed into the little community of Pedro Point, unchanged after more than 40 years. The jumbled houses and bars did not appear to have been painted in all that time. The beach-level road that led to Hidden Cove was blocked by a yellow metal barricade adorned with a sign, "State Property, Access by Permission Only." I turned around and drove to the top of the highest street behind the town. Parking at the top, I walked to the edge of the cliff overlooking Hidden Cove.

With the wind blowing in my face, I thought about the places I had visited today. Looking down to the cove, I remembered Bea and how cold the water was on our feet. As the howl of the wind filled my ears, I remembered the scroll and Mr. Sakai's words when I'd asked permission to marry his daughter.

"I think you will be an asset to our family. Even my very traditional brother, Saburo, who is back in Japan, will come to see that your marriage to Beatrice is a good thing. Saburo may visit Hawaii later this year. Who knows? If things go well for him, maybe he'll be able to make it all the way to the West Coast."

In the years since the end of the war, I'd learned from one of many television histories that a Japanese naval aviator named Saburo Sakai had flown at Pearl Harbor and three days later shot down Colin Kelly's B-17. This awakening was the first test of my willing disbelief that Mr. Sakai could have been an enemy agent. I'd always put it down to coincidence, but now this little-known fact seemed to be the keystone that anchored an arch of suspicion that was building in my mind.

Mr. Sakai's words, spoken to me in approving my marriage to Bea, now fit together in an arch that spanned the Pacific. With the revelation from the scroll that Mr. Sakai had been a spy, I wondered if I was part of a plan that would have been furthered by having a Caucasian son-in-law. Had Bea and I been guided together by Mr. Sakai's unseen hand? Was I simply the Caucasian version of Russell Shimozono?

I felt dirty inside, violated. I didn't know if I had been seduced or raped. Who I was—or thought I was—had been altered forever by what I had done. I had dipped my soul in shit and no amount of scrubbing could remove the stink. I couldn't face living with the unredeemable guilt the small silk scroll had laid upon my soul.

I believed that Bea was unaware of this part of her dad's life. Mrs. Sakai didn't know about her husband, or else she would not have been mentioned on the silk scroll. There were so many victims—both the Sakai family and the men that I may have helped to kill.

Should I find Bea and share what I had learned about her dad? No, my final act of love across so many years and miles would be to keep Mr. Sakai's secret, and not bring any more pain to Bea. Neither time nor the actions of others could minimize what she had meant to me.

In the end, I chose to think of myself as being like Mr. Sakai—a good man capable of doing bad things. If he was a traitor to his adopted country, it was because he was a hero and a patriot to the land of his birth. Pogo's cartoon wisdom made sense to me now; "We have met the enemy and he is us!"

Bea was lost to me long ago. Besides losing her, I'd lost my peace of mind along with whatever innocence I may have possessed. I had been careful as I exacted my vengeance. Maybe I didn't pull off a perfect crime. I just hadn't been caught—at least not yet, anyway.

I could go home to an empty house and wait for a knock at my door because my crime had finally been discovered. When the scope of my crime was realized and the bodies counted, their pursuit would never end. Would someone someday put it all together? The Mark 14 failures, the salted fuel, and who didn't belong in the fuel storage area? The fine bronze dust that showered my shop coat as I worked on the turbine blades would have fallen from my hair, my pants and my hands as I'd salted the fuel drums. I'd signed my work—the phantom grinder—if only they recognized the signature.

How wrong I'd been about Mr. Sakai. My duty and obligation to my county, so long ignored, could no longer be rationalized away. Now, like the Ronin, it was time to satisfy my obligations to the state and to the dead. I'm finally at peace, my mind made up. I sing softly to myself the tune that keeps repeating in my head, "Blue Moon." Then I closed my eyes to better enjoy the music.

The Claxton horn jarred me awake, or did it? Could I be dreaming? Is this what the unborn dream about? Paying their butcher's bill?

Looking down at myself, I'm dressed in blue dungarees and a blue chambray shirt. Before me are lights, dials and switches that I recognize from Mare Island. I look above the array. Affixed to the metal wall that curves up and over my head, is a bronze plaque — USS Grayling.

"Battle stations, torpedo. Target identification please," the captain said.

"Hokuan Maru, troop transport, twelve thousand tons, captain," responded the executive officer as he compared the image in the periscope with the book of vessel identification silhouettes.

"Angle and range on the target, if you please."

"We're close, captain: eight hundred yards at seventeen degrees off the port."

"Make ready two bow tubes, fire at three hundred yards. Running time to the target for those fish?"

"Roger that, coming up to four hundred yards now. Run time to the target twenty-five seconds, sir."

"Helm, get ready to give me full right rudder, as soon as our fish are away."

"Ready on full right, sir."

"Three hundred yards."

"Fire!"

"Two away sir," confirmed the executive officer.

"Time to target?"

"Fifteen seconds...Captain, we've lost the screws on both fish. Dead fish, sir," spoke the sonar man.

"Right full rudder, emergency full down."

"She's on us sir, we're going to get hit," barked the sonar man.

The impact of the troop ship's keel hitting the Grayling came just seconds later. Striking us just behind the conning tower, the keel tore through our hull and rolled the cylindrical submarine completely over, tossing men off their feet. I was thrown against my station's control panel.

Blood began to ooze from my head. Involuntarily I slid along the floor as the angle of our descent steepened and I fought to regain my feet. The Claxton horn, the shouted orders and the yelling of trapped and dying men all mingled as sea water began to flood the conning tower floor. God, the water was cold.

Then the noise stopped. In the total silence I realized that all my companions in the rapidly flooding compartment were staring at me. They knew what I had done.

"I'm sorry," I tried to say but the rising water cut me off. And as we all died together, in my final instant my shipmates never stopped staring at me.

Waking from my daydream to the bright sun, I remembered Walter Cronkite's question. What do the unborn dream about? Do they dream about their sins? Their butcher's bills waiting to be paid?

Living is hard. Dying is easy. As I stand on the edge of the cliff overlooking Hidden Cove, the wind roars and pushes against my chest to keep me away from the edge. Seagulls float on the air currents ten feet from my shoes. I take my final two steps forward, my arms out for flight or crucifixion. It's so beautiful here. My final words, "I love you..." go unheard above the roar of the wind.

THE END

If you enjoyed this book, please do the author and other readers a favour and post a review on Amazon or Goodreads.

If you want to read more about Pat McBride and Mildred, check out Spirit Lake Payback below.

From the Author

Prisoners of War is simultaneously a love story, a mystery and a history, all woven together. Everything of a historical nature is true to the best of my knowledge and research.

The descriptions are drawn from my own family recollections. My mother was a secretary working at the Ellenwood Refinery that was shelled by the Japanese submarine and she was there for the Battle of Los Angeles. My father, besides being a bookmaker and bootlegger, operated a coffee shop amid the piers on San Francisco Bay. He provided the descriptions of those early faux coast defenses.

Both my parents recalled the public's belief, sometimes fostered by the military and the press that in the event of invasion, "We'd stop em' at the Grand Canyon or at the Sierra Nevada mountains."

My Uncle Warren was a railroad man, drafted to the Keyport torpedo works, where he worked in Building 73 as a grinder, perfecting torpedo turbine blades. He was housed in a converted chicken coop.

I grew up in San Bruno near Tanforan racetrack and the Golden Gate National Cemetery, and I attended the annual Posey parade. In high school I worked with an American cousin of Saburo Sakai. I've been to the wonderful museum at Keyport, studied Mark 14 torpedoes and received tremendous assistance from the museum's library staff. Their tip about the antipathy between Newport and Keyport inspired lots of research and, as you have seen, many story elements.

Finally, much of the emotion presented is probably rooted in my actually having received the proverbial 'Dear John' letter while in Air Force basic training and then, years later, being engaged to marry a beautiful oriental woman whose father died in federal prison after being incarcerated for espionage. Our relationship had been supported by her father and opposed by her mother.

About the Author

After returning from the Air Force, Stu Scott worked as staff in a juvenile detention facility, moving on to adult probation and finally to federal probation and parole. Simultaneously, in 1980 he returned to the military as a reserve agent with the Army Criminal Investigation Command. Born and raised in the San Francisco bay area, he has lived with his wife in Moscow, Idaho since 1981. Believing that we only go around once in life and that one job is never enough, his other careers include: professional winemaker, college instructor, director of a school for disabled children and as a stained-glass artist.

sls@turbonet.com

Also By This Author

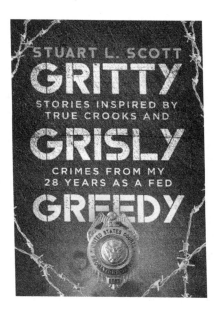

The Tooth Fairy

A story as cold as a Spokane winter about what happens when a crook chooses the wrong victim.

The Grand Tetons

The Texas bank robber who carries twin 38's.

Idaho Catch and Release

Husband and wife pornographers who give a new meaning to what's really a crime.

The Deal

The 1976 case of a crooked politician revisited in 2016.

Available at Amazon in paperback and on Kindle
ISBN:9781732246812

Sample from *Gritty, Grisly, Greedy*

The Grand Tetons

It was a hot August day in 1969 when Janet Lee walked into the center of Clarksville, Texas from where she parked her car in the Seven Eleven lot by the highway. Her hometown in Oklahoma looked just like this one. The square of every small Texas town had either a courthouse or a city hall on one side. Across the square was the bank, and between the two, in the center of the square, was a flagpole with a cannon at its base. The red, white and blue of the Texas flag hung just below Old Glory. With no breeze, the two flags blended into one mass of colors.

"I wonder if this is the Clarksville that The Monkees sang about?" she muttered as she crossed the square. The Walmart that had come to town last year had already driven out many of the local merchants. The storefronts on the square were all empty except for the Farmers and Merchants Bank. That was all she needed. It was more than that. It was a gift, and you could make more of it.

Entering the bank, Janet let her eyes adjust to the interior lighting. A manager sat at a desk in the rear of the lobby. She doodled on a withdrawal slip before taking it over to the lone teller who stood at one of the three stations.

"Hello." She switched on her most dazzling smile, tossed her ash-blond hair and beamed at the young man with her bright blue eyes.

"Good morning, Ma'am." He flushed. "Ar...eh...I mean good afternoon." He finally managed to get out, "How can I help you today?"

"Well thank you." She smiled and passed the withdrawal slip across the counter. "I'd like to make a withdrawal, please."

218

Slowly she opened the front of her short denim jacket, first one side and then the other, to reveal the white fishnet of her tank top. The smile on the face of the young man disappeared. His eyes were drawn to the rose-pink nipples that seemed to be staring at him through the mesh. He tried looking back up to her brilliant smile but couldn't. From her round, firm breasts the rosy nipples were still staring up at his eyes. Then his gaze dropped to the large brown wood gun butt that hugged the flat of her stomach. Some emblem, a Texas star perhaps, was inset on the grip.

"Take all the money from your drawer and put it in the bag, honey." She held eye contact with him, even though his stare had not yet left the gun. She removed a white flour sack from her back pocket and passed it across the counter. "Please don't spoil either of our days by pushing any alarm. Momma needs the money for her surgery, and I'm just trying to be a good daughter."

When the full bag slid back across the counter, she spoke again. "Wait just a bit before you do anything." She did her best to portray both innocence and vulnerability by managing a small frown. Then, buttoning the middle button on her jacket, she walked out of the bank, but not out of his dreams.

*   *   *   *

"So can you tell me what she was wearing?" asked Deputy Sheriff Muldrow, from Red River County.

"Denim jeans and a denim jacket," was the response. The answer from the teller started the deputy writing in his notebook as they sat across the table in the bank's employee lounge.

"What color was her hair?"

"I don't remember." The teller stared at the table, avoiding eye contact with the deputy.

"What about the color of her eyes?"

"I don't remember." The deputy pressed on.

"Did she have a gun?"

"Yes, there was a gun."

At last, they we're back on track. "Okay, what kind of a gun was it?"

"Big gun." He shook his head apologetically.

Trying not to let his frustration show, the deputy tried again. "Is there anything else you can recall?" The teller didn't seem to hear the question. After what seemed like a minute, Muldrow repeated the question.

"She had a beautiful smile. I just couldn't seem to tear my eyes away."

"From her smile?"

"Yes, that's right, from her smile." Then he shut up. He wasn't about to volunteer that all he could recall were her beautiful breasts.

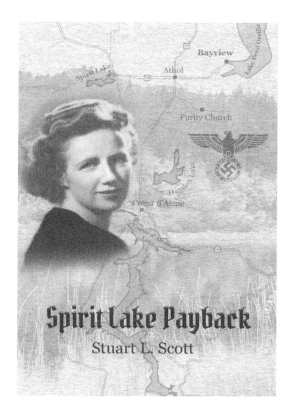

Meet the three women who turn the tables on their victimizers; the bigamist, the rapist and the molester.

"A deceptively slim yet viciously potent slice of female retribution." Kirkus Reviews

Available at Amazon in paperback and on Kindle

ISBN: 978-1-7322468-6-7

Sample from Spirit Lake Payback

Prologue: Spokane, Washington

June 6, 1995

The Spokane newspaper article ran under the banner, **Residents Rush to Plug Leaky Lake.**

"It was only last week that this reporter's boat was in the water, but now it's beached on weeds and mud, here next to my dock. State officials aren't sure why the lake is leaking, but they know it's leaking a lot of water into the Spokane aquifer. The state believes that holes are the main problem. The spokesman for the Idaho Department of Lands explained. 'It's tough to tell legitimate holes from the occasional moose footprint, or one dug by a toad when the lakebed was dry. The trick is to stir up some muck near a suspected hole. If it gets sucked down, the hole is declared a "leaker" and resealed. Unless you see it happen, it's hard to believe.'"

June 10, 1995

Today the follow-up newspaper headline was an eye catcher. **Spirit Lake Sink Hole Collapses to Reveal Skeletal Remains.**

"Idaho authorities interrupted the efforts of local homeowners to seal the continuing plague of sink holes when an undetermined number of human skeletons were discovered in the bottom muck of a collapsed sink hole. A 250 ft. area on the south shore of the lake has been cordoned off. State and tribal archeologists are preparing to excavate the site, hoping to determine the provenance of the apparent ancient burial ground."

June 30, 1995

Spirit Lake Sink Hole Linked to Mob Body Dump.

The Kootenai County Sheriff in his lakeside press conference revealed, "Those remains appear to be 40 to 60 years old and not a tribal burial ground as we first imagined. The archeological excavation has yielded up scraps of clothing and shoes that confirm the approximate age of the remains. The Coeur d'Alene tribal Archeologist called us in yesterday when he removed a skull from the pit and noticed fillings and gold teeth. Once the site is excavated, the identification of the remains will begin. Until that time, we have a bit of a mystery on our hands."

A combined local, state and federal multi-agency task force recovered nine bodies from their Spirit Lake dump site. Skeletal remains had become disarticulated into a pile of anonymous bones, awaiting re-assembly. When they were dumped was a mystery, but bullet holes in many of the skulls and cut marks on bones all pointed to violent ends for the nine unknowns.

Before COVID-19 was the 1918 Spanish Flu. Before that was the 1916 Polio epidemic. New York City had the highest infection rate, but the state with the worst rate was Nevada.

The last US Mail wagon robbery in the country happened in Nevada and the stolen payroll money was never found. To boost his newspaper sales, Joe Pulitzer sent staff West to cover this incident.

Was there a connection?

Available at Amazon in paperback and on Kindle
ISBN: 978-1-7375429-1-9

Sample from Last Ghost Dance

Love and Death in a Small Town

Verrall Black sprang from the swarthy, dark *Reivers* of the Scottish Lowlands, a place of constant border warfare. His beard matched the black of his hair and eyes. He stood 5 foot 9 inches tall, wire tough, the sinews of his forearms bulging beneath their canopy of black hair. His coloration lived on in his oldest daughter, Melba. His second child, Doris, had her mother's red hair and pale skin that would too soon freckle.

The Black family came to Nevada in the 1880s. Verrall Black used the proceeds from his family's success in cattle ranching to open a store in Deeth. The sign above the porch overhang read, "Deeth Mercantile—General Merchandise." The town boasted 500 souls in 1908, and his was the only store. The local Paiute band sold pine nuts and deer hide gloves to the mercantile.

Business was good, supplying the locals from Starr Valley, miners from the gold mines at Jarbidge, and cowboys from The Union Land and Cattle Company that ran over 1000 head of cattle on the sage-covered range surrounding the town.

Across the dirt street from the Mercantile was the Post Office. As the railhead for the Jarbidge mines, Deeth became the largest town in Northern Nevada. Jarbidge gold fueled an expanding local economy.

An opera house, roller rink, barbershop and ice cream parlor opened. Solidifying Deeth as a town was a two-cell city jail, a one-room school, a Chinese laundry and a boarding house and restaurant.

The boarding house was not to be confused with the "Women's Boarding House" that operated above the town's only tavern and dance hall, owned by John Hudson. Cowboys, miners and railroad men now had more opportunities to shed their

burden of heavy gold coins. Three "working ladies," Minnie, Mabel, and Lottie, rented the rooms upstairs. Hudson was their landlord, not their employer.

Lottie Loomis was a willowy brunette from California. She had left her home heading for Denver but only made it as far as Deeth. She had the looks, personality and discipline to do more than trade what she had for what she needed to get by; she aspired to operate a house of her own. She exuded seduction along with raw sexuality. Lottie's real talent was effortlessly convincing men that she wanted them as much as they wanted her. She flirted. She teased. She told every man that found his way into her arms, "You are different from all the men I've known before." Unfortunately, John Hudson believed her.

The saloon owner had set his sights on Lottie. He dreamed about her constantly, in fantasies both erotic and domestic. He took every opportunity to keep her in his sight. Lacking self-esteem, he never risked the rejection, or worse, ridicule by showing his feelings.

John had a hired bartender in the evening, allowing him to float between being a greeter and piano player. As he played his piano below, his mind couldn't escape the thought of Lottie in bed with another man just above him. One Saturday night, he watched Lottie ascend the stairs with a customer, laughing and smiling at the man. His control cracked. His eyes leaked tears as he played the ivory keys. Onward his imagination led him. She was up there now, right above his head, sharing her charms with someone who didn't love her or deserve her as he did.

His hands balled into fist and the fists crashed onto the keyboard. The clang of the keys rang out over the conversations from the barroom and dance floor. As the music stopped, so did the dancers and the talk. The room went silent when John drew out a Colt revolver from his inside coat pocket and began shooting into the dance hall ceiling. "Boom-boom-boom."

No one moved. One group of four men immediately turned their table sideways for a barricade. Ben Kuhl, a small-time thief, had just introduced his two friends, Bob McGinty and Ed Beck, to Fred Searcy, a local teamster. Kuhl believed Fred, who drove a freight wagon, might be a good man to know. He'd file away Searcy's name and his job for possible later use.

The four looked over the table top. Every eye in the room was now focused on Hudson. Adjusting his aim, he let loose again, "boom-boom-boom," emptying his gun into the pale plaster ceiling. The crowd watched as he turned away from the piano and dropped the pistol onto the floorboards at his feet. His elbows went to his knees as he wept into his hands. Drops of smelly liquid began to fall through the bullet holes and drip onto his shirt.

Ed Smiley, the bartender, finally judged it safe to approach his sobbing boss. He picked up the gun, passing it to Dennis McDermott. Ed then walked through the cloud of black powder smoke and climbed the stairs from the dance hall to the bedrooms. From the hallway, the two other doors were cracked open. Other upstairs customers, half-clad, peeked out. The door to Lottie's room was still shut. Ed paused at the door, listening. Finally, he spoke the first words since the shooting. "I'm coming in."

No one was alive inside the small room. Two naked figures lay entangled on the metal-framed bed. Lottie's body lay face down astride her male guest. Blood pooled on the bedding and the floor from two bullet wounds to her upper body. Her companion was shot in the thigh. Other wound tracks, concealed by their bodies, were dripping blood onto the floor. There it mixed with the liquid contents of a chamber pot under the bed, also shot through. The ammonia from urine mixed with the iron smell of their blood.

Ed backed up, closed the door and walked down the stairs to the dance hall.

Hudson was still seated on his piano stool, head in hands. Word had spread out from the bar to the de facto leaders of the town. Verrall Black, Ben Armstrong and Bob Anderson clustered together with Dennis McDermott in the center of the room.

Ed took two steps toward the men before speaking. "Lottie and Roy Wooden, the section foreman, are both dead." Standing aside as the four men whispered among themselves, Smiley posed the unspoken question on many minds. "What's to be done now?"

Verrall Black spoke for the group. "We've been talking it over. Ben and Bob will take Hudson over to the jail for the night. We'll ask Mabel and Minnie to clean up Lottie's body and wind her tight in a sheet. You and I will do the same for Roy."

"Then what?" asked Ed.

"You get some help, maybe the other men upstairs, and move the two bodies to the cattle company shed for now. That will keep them cold and safe until somebody comes up from Elko."

Smiley nodded his agreement. The five men separated to deal with their appointed tasks. Hudson's shirt was soaked by the drops falling from above. Fate had pissed on him again.

As they separated, one of the group turned and stopped the bartender with a question." Did she know how he felt?"

"I guess not."

Later Saturday night, Verrall and Ed Smiley took two blankets, a plate of biscuits and stew, hard candy and a cup of hot coffee over to John Hudson. They had no concerns about Hudson trying to escape.

"John, these should help you through the night. There's a slop bucket under the bunk. You may have already found that."

Hudson nodded that he had. He sat on the wooden bunk, staring at the cement floor, but neither spoke nor made eye contact with Black.

Verrall nudged Hudson with the plate and offered the hot cup of coffee. Hudson took both as Ed Smiley entered the cell and placed the blankets on the bunk.

As the cell door closed, Hudson looked up and gave a momentary smile. "Thank you." After a long pause, he spoke again. "They're dead, aren't they." It was not a question.

Ed Smiley delivered the answer as the cell door closed. "Yes. Both."

In the morning, John Hudson was dead by his own hand, hung with an improvised noose fashioned from strips of blankets braided together and attached to bars in the cell window. His meager last meal lay untouched on the bunk.

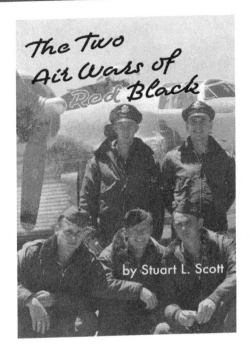

The wartime adventures of William "Red" Black, with just
enough fiction to connect the true events.
He went from a childhood on a chicken farm in Stockton,
California to navigating a B-24 over Europe. Shot down over
Germany, he escaped to Sweden.
He stayed in the service after WWII.
"Lieutenant Black, what would you like to do, now?"
"Not being able to shoot back is bullshit.
I want to be a fighter pilot!"
He flew an F-82 Twin Mustang night fighter
in the Korean War.
Discover the untold costs of war on a man who chose to defend
us all.

Available at Amazon in paperback and on Kindle
ISBN 978-1-7375429-1-9

Made in the USA
Monee, IL
20 July 2023

39398558R00134